TREASURE AND PROTECT

BOOK SEVEN IN THE HEROES OF EVERS,
TEXAS SERIES

LORI RYAN

OTHER BOOKS BY LORI RYAN

The Sutton Billionaires Series:

The Billionaire Deal

Reuniting with the Billionaire

The Billionaire Op

The Billionaire's Rock Star

The Billionaire's Navy SEAL

Falling for the Billionaire's Daughter

The Sutton Capital Intrigue Series:

Cutthroat

Cut and Run

Cut to the Chase

The Sutton Capital on the Line Series:

Pure Vengeance

Latent Danger

The Triple Play Curse Novellas:

Game Changer

Game Maker

Game Clincher

The Heroes of Evers, TX Series:

Love and Protect

Promise and Protect

Honor and Protect (An Evers, TX Novella)

Serve and Protect

Desire and Protect

Cherish and Protect

Treasure and Protect

The Dark Falls, CO Series:

Dark Falls

Dark Burning

Dark Prison

Coming Soon – The Halo Security Series:

Dulce's Defender

Hannah's Hero

Shay's Shelter

Callie's Cover

Grace's Guardian

Sophie's Sentry

Sienna's Sentinal

For the most current list of Lori's books, visit her website:
loriryanromance.com.

CHAPTER ONE

CORA WALKER WASN'T a stupid woman, but it was beginning to dawn on her that she *was* foolish at times.

Now was one of those times.

She had just caught herself fantasizing about Justin Kensington. Again.

She wondered if she'd ever get past her inane obsession with the blond-haired god. Sure, he had the kind of body that made you want to lick him like a lolly-pop, and yes, his eyes were mesmerizing in the extreme, but still. She should have more control than this, shouldn't she?

When he walked into the diner while she was waiting for her friend Laura Kensington to arrive, she'd caught herself imagining he might walk up to her. Instead of seeing the reality—which had been him saying hello to Presley and James across the room—she'd pictured him ignoring all the greetings from friends as he walked through the room to get to her. That kind of intense, single-minded focus you saw on a man's face in a movie when he saw the woman he wanted across a crowded room.

When he reached her, he'd put out his hand and draw

her up from the table, then step into her space, standing just inside the line that said they were more than friends. He'd put one arm around her waist, letting his hand slide along her hip and around to her back. He'd press her to him, blue eyes sparkling with heat, and bend to whisper a personal hello in her ear.

She often had fantasies like this about Justin, despite the fact that he'd shown her time and again he had no interest in her other than as a friend.

Her sister was the romance novelist in the family. Somehow, Ashley always came up with these steamy, suspenseful plots filled with twists and turns that boggled Cora's mind. If Cora was writing a romantic suspense, she'd have lame little narrations, like: *in a stupidly handy turn of events, the heroine stumbled on a loaded weapon and turned to fire at her pursuer. She was a miraculously good shot for someone with no experience with a gun.*

Yeah, Cora wasn't an author for a reason. But with her fantasies about Justin, Cora could have given Ashley a run for her money.

They'd be at a party and she'd invent scenes where Justin drew her into a closet and stripped her bare, whispering for her to be quiet as he ravished her. In another, he'd dropped his beer bottle and lifted her so he could set her on a nearby table to kiss her properly.

"Properly" being with her legs and arms wrapped around him as he ground between her thighs.

She was welcomed back to the real world when Justin slid into the seat across from her.

"Hey, Cora. Meeting someone?" His dimples got her every time. He was like Robert Redford back in the '70s when he was super hot, only modern, not wearing shirts with big collars unbuttoned halfway to his knees.

Not that she'd mind his shirt unbuttoned halfway to his knees.

She mentally slapped herself. "Laura. We're having lunch."

Our heroine has resorted to stating the painfully obvious in an attempt at witty repartee with the hero.

He grinned at her.

"We have lunch sometimes," she mumbled. Lord, she couldn't stop herself.

Gina, one of the two sisters who owned and ran Two Sisters diner came to the table giving Cora the reprieve she badly needed.

"Still waitin' on one more?" she asked. Cora had already told her she was waiting for Laura.

"I can't stay. Tina's making me a sandwich to go," Justin said, with a nod of his head toward Tina, the other sister, who could be seen through the pass-through window that led to the kitchen.

It wasn't a surprise. When Justin first came to town, people hardly saw him. He stayed holed up in his house or office all the time. If you did see him, he wore a scowl that warned people away. Nowadays, he smiled more and he had friends, but he still worked much of the time. There was also a bit of the scowl left in him. It wasn't always on his face, but it was there. It was almost like he carried a heaviness with him wherever he went.

"That's a pretty necklace, Gina," Cora said. She leaned in. The necklace was heart shaped with small gems of various colors studding the heart.

Gina blushed, a hand going to the jewelry on her neck. "Thank you. The General got it for me."

No one had to ask who the General was. General Brophy came to town frequently nowadays, both to visit his daughter, Phoebe Joy, who was dating Shane Bishop, and to see his favorite waitress, Gina.

When Gina had moved on to a table across the room, Justin leaned in. "Do you think she calls him General in—"

Cora slapped her hands over her ears. "Don't say it. You're horrible!"

"What's horrible?" Laura asked, plopping herself on the seat next to Cora.

Justin was laughing as he got up and walked away.

Laura looked to Cora. "What did I miss?"

"You don't want to know." She searched for another topic. "Did you hear that Ron Knight filed his lawsuit?" The whole town had known the suit was coming.

"I did." Laura switched her seat to sit across from Cora now that Justin was gone. "I heard everyone talking about it the minute I walked through the door."

Two Sisters Diner was not only in the center of town physically, it was the center of town gossip. Cora didn't doubt that everyone there was talking about Mr. Knight and his lawsuit.

She sighed. "I'll find out how he's doing later today." She'd started visiting him on Sundays when he'd been diagnosed with a rare type of cancer. She hadn't stopped when he started telling everyone that Caufield Furniture had made him sick by mishandling the chemicals they used at an old storage facility near his land.

Sadly, his suit against the company was upsetting a lot of people. The company was one of the major employers in the area. People had depended on it for their livelihoods for decades. Seeing it threatened wasn't going over all that well, even if people felt for Mr. Knight and his neighbors, who'd all been diagnosed with significant illnesses.

Cora watched Justin pay for his sandwich and walk out.

She knew he would be going back to the offices of the nonprofit he ran with Laura. He worked most weekends.

"Can I ask you something?" Cora asked, refocusing on Laura.

"Always."

"Do you think a person can just decide to get over someone they've been hung up on for a long time?"

Laura didn't try to pretend she didn't know who they were talking about. "I'd like to think he's going to wake up one of these days and see what he's missing. I happen to think you guys would be great together."

Laura was more than a friend of Justin's. Justin was her former husband's brother and they worked closely together running the nonprofit they'd started. If anyone knew Justin, it was Laura.

"I sense a but coming," Cora said.

"But," Laura said, with emphasis, "Justin has some issues and I don't know when he's going to get past those."

"Yeah," Cora said. She slumped down in her seat, sipping her club soda.

Laura tilted her head. "Can I ask you something now?"

"Always," Cora said, mimicking her friend's earlier response.

"Do you think you've been waiting all this time for him to notice you because you want him, or do you think maybe you're focused on him because he's unattainable and you know it?"

Laura's words were soft but they cut just as if she'd put venom behind them.

Cora's denial was immediate. "Of course not."

Laura waited.

Cora laughed at her. "Really, it's not. I mean, that makes no sense."

There was no denying Laura was perceptive. She'd been taught to read other's emotions at a high cost during her previous marriage. Still, she was wrong here.

They were interrupted briefly when Gina came to take their orders, but Laura didn't let the subject drop. "Just think about it. It's just that, sometimes, people who have lost people early on in their lives do things to make sure they don't have to go through that again."

Cora was silent but she would be lying if she said Laura's suggestion didn't stick with her through the rest of the meal.

Even though her gut response had been that Laura was wrong, some part of her wondered if her friend might be right. Maybe it was time for a little more soul searching instead of just pouting over the fact her crush clearly saw her as nothing more than a friend. A completely platonic, asexual friend.

CHAPTER TWO

JUSTIN TOSSED his keys onto the desk in his office and looked at the stack of mail waiting for him. He had planned to eat his sandwich while he worked his way through the pile, but the idea held little appeal now.

He wanted something, but he didn't know what. Something to take the edge off.

Cora Walker smiling and laughing as he joked with her came to mind.

Yeah, Cora would take the edge off.

Not an option.

He tossed his sandwich on the desk and pulled his shirt off over his head. There was no one in the office with him and the door to the building was locked. He'd do some pushups to burn off the energy skittering through him.

He hit the floor of his office, trying to shut down his mind, focusing instead on the sound of the count in his head. *One, two, three, four, five.*

Sweet red lips curved into a tempting smile.

He shut the image out.

It had taken all his will to stay away from Cora Walker for the last three years. As far as their friends were concerned, her interest in him was one-sided. It was far from that, but since he wouldn't act on his attraction under any circumstances, it would be unwise to let his feelings show.

He growled as he added a clap between each pushup. The impromptu workout wasn't doing shit to blot her out of his mind, but it had taken the edge off a little. He might be able to focus if he kept this up a while longer. He'd be sweaty and grungy, but he'd get his focus back.

———

CORA WALKED through town after lunch, heading for her duplex so she could start on the muffins she'd take to Mr. Knight later that day.

She turned when she got to Elm Street, though, veering off and heading for the park.

It hadn't come as any surprise when Laura referred to her childhood loss. Her background wasn't a great mystery. The histories of the Walker kids were no secret. The main details were known by everyone in town.

People might not know what it was like for her as a six-year-old kid to wait on a park swing where her mom had left her. They wouldn't know the panic she'd experienced when darkness fell and her mom didn't return.

But they all knew the rough details of the story. That she'd been found by a stranger who took her to the police. That her mom had never returned. That her mom hadn't cared enough to even leave her in a safe place like outside a hospital or at a fire station.

Cora stood now, in front of the park swings. This wasn't

the park her mom had left her in, but it was close enough to dredge up the memories.

As if some unseen force took hold of her body, she moved forward and sat on the nearest swing.

Her feet reached the ground now.

She took her phone out, pulling up an internet browser and typing in the phrase: abandonment issues. She'd gone to therapy. She knew what issues she might face as an adult, but she'd honestly thought she'd defeated all of them. She didn't think she was affected the way she might have been if she hadn't been adopted by the Walkers.

There was a bitter taste in her mouth as she remembered how bad things had been the year before when the full revelations of Ashley's history had come out. Cora hadn't ever overtly thought the words, but some small piece of her had been grateful she'd dodged the bullet of the emotional scars Ashley had borne.

Maybe she'd just never realized she was scarred.

She looked at the list of things someone who had been abandoned as a child might do.

Jumping from relationship to relationship. She laughed. She certainly hadn't been doing any of that. Her dating life had been nonexistent lately.

Looking for flaws in every partner. What partners?

Attaching too quickly.

Settling for unhealthy relationships. Again, what relationships?

Being overly controlling or jealous. Nope.

Choosing unavailable partners.

Oh.

Cora frowned as she looked at the last one in the list and wondered if Laura had read it.

She went on to read about people who were so frightened of being left, they made sure they didn't get into a position where someone could leave.

She had close friends, family who loved her, people in her world she trusted to be there. Still, she had to admit, she hadn't ever had a serious boyfriend. She hadn't dated a ton, but the men she'd dated just hadn't turned out to be the one for her, right?

She remembered the way one of her exes laughed and joked about not being ready for a ball and chain. Another had always said there was no need to talk about marriage before the two-year anniversary. At the time, she had thought when they fell in love, they'd change their minds. She thought she was mature for not worrying about it before then. They hadn't fallen in love, though.

Maybe, on some level, the way her past boyfriends had resisted marriage had been a comfort for her. If they didn't get married, she wouldn't have to worry that he might someday decide he didn't want her. That they would someday want to end that marriage.

She closed the browser feeling a little sick as she began to question just how mentally healthy she'd been all these years, then opened it again, this time navigating to a search page. She entered: *internet dating*, and scrolled through the online dating options.

She didn't know if Laura was right about her wanting Justin because she knew on some level that he wasn't available. Maybe it was nothing more than a coincidence that several of her boyfriends had been vocal about not wanting to get married yet.

She didn't know, but she did know she didn't want to feel this way anymore. She didn't want to be the one at the party who wasn't part of a couple. Whatever her reasons for being attracted to Justin, it was time to put a stop to it because it was clear, Justin Kensington wasn't into her and she would have to be an idiot to keep telling herself, *maybe someday*.

CHAPTER THREE

JUSTIN WALKED into Pies and Pints, wondering why he'd let Laura talk him into coming out. She'd been getting on him to hire a deputy director at the foundation they ran together, arguing he worked too much.

She thought Justin was a martyr, trying to work himself into the ground to make up for the fact he hadn't known she was being abused when she was married to his brother. He'd heard the lecture just the other day. It didn't mean it made it any easier to find the right deputy director for the center. Still, convincing her of that seemed like a lost cause.

Laura was over by the two dart boards with most of their other friends. His eyes automatically scanned the group for the brown-eyed woman with the chocolate hair he wanted to see, but Cora didn't seem to be among them.

"Hey," Cade said, handing Justin a mug and filling it with the pitcher of beer that sat on the table. "She's not here."

He wondered if he could deny any knowledge of who Cade was talking about, but Cade's brother, Shane, came up on the other side of him and leaned in.

"She's on a date."

Justin raised his mug and forced himself to swallow. Apparently, it wasn't worth trying to deny who he was looking for.

He found the entire group looking at him. In addition to Laura and her second husband, Cade, there was Cade's brother, Shane, and his girlfriend, Phoebe. Ashley—Cora's older sister—and her husband, Garret, were also there.

Justin scowled. "What do we know about the guy she's out with? How did she meet this guy?"

Ashley snorted. "Subtle. But, yeah, the guy's probably safe. He's a teacher three towns over. She met him online."

Justin felt his jaw drop. "So he says. People can say anything online."

Laura laughed at him, too. "They're meeting in public. I'm sure she's fine."

"Besides," Ashley said, "She's checking in by text with us every hour. If she misses a check-in, we'll go SWAT on her and breach the restaurant."

"Really?" Justin asked, looking around. "You have her checking in every hour?" He could get on board with a plan like that.

"No, dumbass," Cade said, shaking his head. "She's on a date. She's fine."

Cora's voice came from behind him. "No, she's not."

The group turned to stare at her, but Justin was probably the only one who felt the kick to the gut at the sight of her. She was wearing a short purple skirt that had him thinking up too many damned ways to get it off and a white shirt that showed the outline of a purple lacy tank top underneath it.

Then her words registered. "You're not on a date or

you're not okay?" he asked. If her date had done something to her, Justin would have to hunt the man down.

Cora waved a dismissive hand. "I'm fine. Just not on a date."

She looked ready to be on a date. The guy was missing out.

"What happened?" Ashley came forward, putting her arm around her sister's waist and drawing her over to the table where Shane offered her a beer. She shook her head, no, to the drink and stole her sister's water glass.

"Lice," Cora said, making a face. "It's going around his school. He started itching just as we sat down at the restaurant."

Ashley took a large step away from Cora and made her own face.

Cora swatted at her sister. "I don't have it. I use coconut shampoo and conditioner."

"Huh?" Ashley said.

Cora sighed. "Lice hate coconut. You use coconut shampoo and conditioner to prevent them from wanting to set up shop on your head. It's not foolproof, but it helps."

"And your date from hell didn't know this?" Shane asked.

Cora scowled. "He wasn't a date from hell. He seemed..." she paused a little longer than she should have, "nice."

"Absent the bugs on his head," Shane teased.

Phoebe squeezed Shane's arm. "Leave her alone. It can happen to anyone."

Cora didn't look convinced, but she didn't answer.

Justin only half listened as the rest of the group began talking about work weeks and plans for the rest of the weekend. He moved around to where Cora stood and nodded toward the dart boards.

"Darts?"

She looked to the boards, then to him. "You haven't heard?"

"Heard what?"

She leaned a little closer. "I've been banned."

"Excuse me?" He looked around. "By who?"

Were there dart police he didn't know about?

She gestured with her mug to the rest of the group and Ashley must have heard the conversation because she cut in. "She hit me with a dart in the back. Broke the skin. She's not allowed to play anymore."

"I was tipsy," Cora argued, but she gave Justin a smile that said she knew the argument was weak. Cora was horrible at darts, regardless of the effects of alcohol.

He grabbed her arm and tugged her toward the board. Their group had already gotten the darts from the bartender. "I can handle the risk."

Cora shrugged. "It's your body. If you don't mind turning it into a sieve, I don't mind playing." Her grin was infectious as she lifted the first dart and made a show of lining up her shot.

He enjoyed the show. To most people, Cora Walker was the sweet girl who was always ready to help anyone who needed her. She was the one you could count on to volunteer for any fundraiser, to organize meal chains when someone was sick or had a baby, and to pick you up on the side of the road if you had a flat.

To him, she was the sweet girl with the hot body he'd never have the right to put his hands on. Not that he didn't also love the fact she was always there for anyone who needed her. He did. But, still, he had a feeling he appreciated her body a lot more than the women on the church's community volunteer league did.

He knew she felt the same attraction he did. When he first moved to town, she hadn't tried to cover her feelings. Cora was like that. She wore her heart on her sleeve.

But when he'd gently steered them toward friendship instead of anything more, she'd started to try to cover her feelings. She sucked at it.

And judging by the way his friends had made clear they knew what he felt for her, so did he. Luckily, he was better at making sure they never acted on those feelings. That was the one thing he needed to be sure he never let slip.

She tossed her dart, giving a little cheer when she hit the double ring on the outer edge of the board. She threw the other two darts with as much preparation, but neither hit the board. It really was remarkable how bad she was given the fact most of the group spent at least one or two nights a week here. She should really be better at this.

"You're not drinking?" he asked, as she came back, then made the mistake of taking a sip of his own beer before she answered.

"It's not that time of the month."

The beer that had been in his mouth went down the wrong way, making him choke.

She pounded on his back.

He knew Cora only drank once a month. It was part of her effort to control the pieces of her world that her birth mother hadn't. Her birth mother had been an alcoholic. The alcohol had controlled her mother. Cora was determined never to let it get that kind of hold on her.

Still, hearing her flippantly refer to it as "that time of the month" had thrown him off. Then again, Cora often threw him off.

She was grinning at him like she knew exactly what she'd done.

He turned away, choosing to focus on the dart boards instead of flirting back. He didn't know why they did this to themselves. He took a second to line up his shot, feeling the weight of the dart balanced between his fingers before letting it fly. Bullseye.

When he turned, he found Cora standing close behind him, studying his dart where it sat in the green circle of the outer bullseye. She was mimicking the move he'd made when he felt the balance of the dart.

She squinted one eye in concentration for a minute, but then seemed to realize he was watching and she stepped back with a start.

He turned back to the board and fired off the next two shots. Triple ring for both. Great, her bad skill at darts was wearing off on him.

Hell, he thought. It had nothing to do with skill. She was getting to him, distracting him. She always had.

They played in silence for a few more minutes, but his thoughts went to her reasons for drinking once a month.

He knew about her history. The whole town knew each of the Walker siblings had a dark past.

Sam and Emma had been the first to be adopted by the Walkers. They had survived a car accident that took their parents' lives. When the Walkers, who were old friends of their parents, found out about the accident, they got the kids out of foster care and, eventually, adopted them.

Ashley's birth mother had never really been fit to parent. She was left to a foster system that had let her down in a big way, until the Walkers adopted her at fourteen.

Cora's birth mother was an alcoholic who left her in a park when she was little. She never came back.

The story still made him boil with anger. He focused on his breathing for a few seconds, making sure the anger wasn't able to boil to the surface. He'd spent time studying with a Zen priest in the Himalayas when he was twenty-six. It had paid off.

Justin passed the darts to Cora, ignoring the brush of her fingers against his hand.

She took the darts then shook out her arms and bent her head from side to side.

He couldn't help but smirk as she did it. She looked like she was prepping for an Olympic competition.

The first dart flew. It flew straight to the board of the people playing next to them. Cora simply raised a hand in apology and collected her dart when they paused their game for her. Apparently, no one in town expected her to stick to her own board.

When she turned to smile at him as she came back to their side of the lane, he raised a hand, waving to welcome her back. She shrugged and broadened her smile, a glint of mischief and humor lighting her gaze. She was flirting with him.

As he watched her throw the next dart and miss the board again, every inch of him itched to walk up behind her and press his body to hers. To wrap his arms around her and take hold of her hands. It would be so easy to guide her hands as she lined up the dart. He knew if he did that, her ass would press into him, he'd be able to feel every shift her body made as he helped her aim. Every breath she took as they lined up.

Hell, he wouldn't even need all of that. A single touch would be enough. Just resting his hand on her hip as he guided her. That would be heaven. Heaven and hell all at once.

Christ. He stood off the stool he'd been sitting on and tugged on his jeans, hoping no one noticed he was half hard.

The thunk of the dart hitting the board let him know she'd thrown her last dart while he'd been busy fantasizing about her.

"What's the score?" he asked as she turned and brought the darts to him for her turn.

"I think I'm winning," she offered as she slid onto her bar stool, playfully taunting him. "Don't worry, you've got time for a comeback."

He laughed. "Yeah? I'll have to work on that."

He tossed his darts easily, one after the other, earning two more bullseyes and a sixty-point hit.

"No need to show off about it," she grumbled, as she came forward to take the darts from his hand.

He noticed the couples in their group had split off to play pool or dance on the almost nonexistent dance floor of the bar.

He and Cora often ended up paired off like this when they were out with the group. For a long time, he'd told himself that was why people seemed to want to push them together. Now, he knew it was more than that. No one could miss the chemistry between them.

It didn't mean he was going to do anything about it. Justin had realized the men in his family were poison. His father had abused his mother and his brother had abused Laura. Justin had been oblivious to all of it, sticking his head in the sand as he partied on the family's dime in every location around the globe other than his home. He had no business putting any woman at risk by getting involved with them. Least of all a woman with a heart like Cora's.

She threw her next few darts and returned to him.

When she offered the darts to him, he took her wrist

instead, then pulled the darts from them with his other hand.

"You're breaking for summer soon, right?"

She blinked at him, as though surprised by the topic. "Yes."

"Do you have plans for the summer yet?" He knew she'd worked at a local summer camp the last few years, but he thought Ashley mentioned Cora didn't plan to do that this summer.

"Not yet. I'm running a robotics club for some of the students. I'd like to do more for them over the summer, but I need to make some money. I might just offer tutoring and see if I can pick up some hours at the book store."

He studied her. "Have you ever thought of applying for grants to teach summer sessions for your students?"

She took the darts out of his hand. "You forfeit your turn. You're taking too long."

Her dart hit the wall three feet to the right of the board. Two more inches and it would have gone around the corner to where the dance floor sat.

"Grants?" She turned to him, not in the least bit concerned that she could have taken out Norma Vance's shaking booty on the dance floor.

Justin crossed his arms. "It's too late for this summer, but I bet we could find something to apply for next year. It could be for your robotics group so you're actually paid a fair wage for teaching it, or for something else. I'm sure there's money out there somewhere for that sort of thing."

Justin didn't know when the idea had formed in his head, but he liked the sound of it more and more. He could help her look for the grants, then write up the applications.

She didn't bother to pull the darts out of the wall. "Do you have time for that?"

"I can make time." He grinned. "Just say yes. It'll be easier on us both for you to give in now."

She scowled. "Maybe."

"Laura," he said over his shoulder. "Tell Cora she should let me help her write grant proposals for summer programming for her students."

"Absolutely!" Laura called out, as she waited her turn at the pool table.

"See?" He said.

Cora tilted her head. "She isn't even paying attention to anything other than the way her husband's ass looks bent over the pool table and you know it."

"Uh-huh. She has faith that whatever I ask deserves an 'absolutely' for an answer."

She rolled her eyes. "Fine. You can help me find money for my students."

He stuck out his hand, shaking it when she slipped her soft hand into his. "Deal."

He waited until she went to collect the darts again. "So, lice, huh?"

She glared over her shoulder. "It happens."

"Uh-huh."

"Shut up and play. I have a title to defend."

Justin tossed his darts, not much caring where they landed. They hit the board. "It can be a little dangerous, meeting a guy you don't know, don't you think?"

She didn't answer him.

Justin ran a hand through his hair and looked at her. He cared a lot about Cora. Her safety mattered to him. A lot.

"Look, I'm just saying it can be dangerous. When is your next date?"

He was getting into dangerous territory. If he didn't

know it himself already, the look on her face would have told him.

"That's a little personal, don't you think?" She slammed her hands on her hips and he guessed the darts game was forgotten now.

Justin looked over her shoulder to see that none of their friends had noticed them arguing. Good. The last thing he needed was more people seeing what an ass he was, but he couldn't help himself. He wanted to be sure she understood the risks of going out to meet someone she didn't know, even if she did stick to public locations.

With the kind of drugs men could get their hands on nowadays, it would be all too easy for someone to slip something in her drink and walk her out of a restaurant or bar as though she'd simply had one too many drinks.

"Maybe I care." It was the wrong thing to say. He knew that, but it didn't mean he could stop himself.

Her eyes flashed with the anger that seemed to make her body rigid as she came toe-to-toe with him. Her words were softly spoken, but far from gentle. In fact, they seemed to come flying at him through gritted teeth, and he almost wondered how she got them out.

Worse, though, was the look of hurt that accompanied the anger.

"If you cared so much, Justin, you should have done something about it months ago."

He sighed. "Yeah."

He got that.

The anger seemed to go out of her and only the deflated hurt was left. "Yeah," she echoed.

She took the darts from his hand and turned back to the board. Too forgiving of him, as always.

———

CORA BEGAN to stew again on the way home, but by the time she unlocked her front door, she had gone from stewing to feeling deflated. She hated the fact that she still wanted Justin, even when he was butting into her love life. And she hated the fact that her date had gone so badly.

When she'd seen her date waiting for her at the restaurant, she'd known she wasn't going to feel much for him, even before the lice incident. He seemed like a nice guy and he was good looking, but he didn't make her skin feel all tingly or her stomach get all jittery the way Justin did.

She sat on her couch and texted her friend, Julia. She and Julia had started teaching the same year at Evers Elementary. Julia taught pre-k and Cora taught first grade, but their classrooms were across the hall from each other.

Cora: *Dating sucks.*

Julia: *Oh no! What happened? The Get Over My Man Plan isn't working?*

Cora had come up with the brilliant idea to use online dating to get over her crush on Justin. They'd dubbed it the *Get Over My Man Plan.* She let her head fall back on the couch. What had she been thinking, saying she'd work with him on grants? It was sabotage, that's what it was. She was sabotaging herself.

No, she thought to herself. She wasn't stupid. It was the effect of her mother's abandonment on her. It meant that Cora would always have issues with saying goodbye to people and walking away when she should.

Some part of her would always be the six-year-old swinging her legs on a park swing, trying to convince herself that her mom would be back.

She felt like she did that a lot in her life. Waited for love.

That had been evident tonight. As soon as she saw Justin in the bar, she'd slipped right back into flirting with him.

She lifted her head and texted back.

Cora: *Lice.*

Julia's response came in the form of a phone call.

"Hey," Cora answered, heading to the kitchen to see if she had any ice cream.

Jackpot. Caramel swirl. Thank the gods of frozen goods for caramel swirl.

"Okay, lady, I know what you're doing." Julia's words made Cora pull the phone from her ear and look at it, as though she expected to see her friend's face peering through it.

"Yeah? You can see through phones now?" She felt like she was channeling Ashley more and more lately. Ashley was the snarky sister. Cora was supposed to be the good girl. The sweet girl.

"You're eating ice cream and telling yourself you can't do this online dating thing."

"Maybe," she said around a mouthful of caramel goodness.

"Ha!" Julia laughed. "Fine. Let yourself eat the ice cream, but promise me, you'll get off the phone and go check your dating profile. Schedule two more dates or email five new guys. One or the other."

"Ugh."

"You know I'm right," Julia offered in a sing-song voice.

"It doesn't make you any more likable right now," Cora threw back at her, employing the same sing-song.

She was laughing, though, by the time they hung up.

She didn't tell Julia she'd agreed to work for Justin over the summer. She wasn't up to confessions of a Justin Kensington addict right now.

She took her ice cream over to her desk where her laptop sat. Julia was right. She needed to get back in the saddle.

Oh, but not with that guy, she thought, as she hid the profile of a guy who had stalker potential written all over him.

"See, I can say goodbye to people. Goodbye Creepy McCreeperson," she said as she hid another guy's profile. He looked to be about twelve years old.

She hit the *wave hello* button on two guys who had potential and wrote a quick, *sorry-I-don't-play-for-your-team-but-you-look-lovely-and-best-of-luck-to-you* message to a woman the service had accidentally suggested for her.

Her phone pinged with an incoming text.

Julia: *Two dates! No slacking.*

Cora groaned and filled her spoon again as she pulled up the messages section of the website. There had been a few guys she emailed earlier in the week. She could arrange coffee dates with them. Julia hadn't ever said the dates had to be for dinner.

Her phone pinged.

Julia: *Coffee's not a date.*

Hell.

CHAPTER FOUR

CORA COULD HEAR the shuffling footsteps of Mr. Knight as she waited on his front porch. In the last month alone, he seemed to have slowed down considerably.

"It's me, Mr. Knight," she called out as she heard him coming closer.

"Cora?" He asked as he swung the door wide.

His home was out on what used to be one large ranch that had been run by his family for generations. Now, much of the land had been parceled off and a few homes stretched out on either side. The cattle that had once been a staple on the land was gone.

She smiled when he got the door open and held up the basket of muffins. Yes, it was cliché, but she brought muffins to the man whenever she came to see him.

He gave her a mock scowl. "Blueberry, I hope?"

"Of course," she said, following him inside. He seemed to shrink further and further into himself as the days wore on and she worried that he didn't have a lot of support in the town.

In a small town like Evers, when you sued one of the

town's biggest employers, it tended to make people wonder where your loyalties stood.

Cora could understand people being upset about Mr. Knight's suit against Caufield's Furniture, but she also thought his allegations that the company had poisoned his well and was making him sick were worth looking into. Last she heard, his well had been tested and they were testing the soil and the wells of the surrounding properties. Two of the kids on the neighboring land had been diagnosed with cancer in the last two years.

People in the town were sympathetic to what was happening to them, but they were also fiercely aware that the furniture company provided a living for a great many people around here. If the illnesses were nothing more than coincidence, no one wanted to see the company take the fall for it.

Cora followed Mr Knight into the kitchen and watched as he lowered himself into a seat at the table. He began pulling the top off one of the muffins. She did the same thing when she ate a muffin. Top first, because it was the best part, then the bottom.

She heard the front door open again and looked to Mr. Knight with raised brows.

"My son," he said. "Came home to stay with me. He's broke."

"I'm not broke, dad," a man with a broad chest and light brown hair said, as he walked into the room. "I moved home to help you."

He set a stack of boxes on the table and turned to Cora, smiling a smile that held a few crooked teeth. Something about that imperfection made him all the more appealing. He was only an inch or so taller than she was, but he was muscular and had the look of a man who worked for his living. Brown eyes greeted her from a tanned face.

He stuck out a calloused hand. "I'm Ethan Knight. I don't think we've met. I was a few years ahead of you in high school, but everyone knows who the Walkers are."

Cora took his hand. It was warm, his grip firm. She vaguely remembered him, although he'd never exactly been on her radar. Cora's sister, Ashley, had been a trouble maker in high school. If the legends about Ethan Knight were true, he'd made Ashley look like an angel.

"Hi. I'm Cora Walker. But I guess you know that."

Mr. Knight slid the basket of muffins toward his son. "Cora brings me muffins. You only get one."

Ethan grinned and winked at Cora. "I'm probably lucky he's sharing any with me at all."

"You bet your ass you are." Mr. Knight snatched the basket back as soon as Ethan had claimed his allotted snack.

"I can bring more if it's going to cause a fight," Cora said, only half joking.

Ethan changed to a stage whisper. "I'll steal another one when he takes his nap."

Cora found herself smiling again. She gestured to the boxes. "Still moving in?"

The inner narrator of her lame romantic novels chimed in. *Our heroine couldn't come up with anything witty so she went with the inanely bland box conversation.*

"Oh, no," Ethan said. "Those are for work. I do imprinting on promotional items for businesses and things."

"Had to close his store," his dad said around a mouthful of food. Cora was glad to see him eating. He'd been losing a lot of weight lately, and some days he didn't seem to have much of an appetite. She had a feeling that as much as he was complaining about having Ethan there, the change was a positive one.

"I wanted to do it, Dad." Ethan shook his head, but explained to Cora. "I had a shop in San Marcos, but that drive is too far with my dad being sick, so I moved things here. I can do my printing just as well here and ship things to my clients."

His dad snorted like he was talking to a child Ethan instead of the adult version in front of him.

"That Derrick Ayers came by while you were out. You tell him I don't want him coming around here." Mr. Knight crossed his arms over his chest, sticking out his chin. At one time, the move had probably been intimidating, at least to his son. Not so much anymore.

Ethan sighed. "Dad, I haven't hung out with Derrick Ayers in years, but I don't have any control over him if he comes around to say hi. He probably just heard I was back in town."

"That boy is no good."

Cora didn't want to stick around for the rest of the conversation. "I have to get going, Mr. Knight. I'm due out at my parent's house in a bit for dinner." She turned to Ethan. "It was great meeting you, Ethan."

"I'll walk you out," he said and walked by her side, his hands shoved in his pockets as they moved through the house to the front door.

He walked her all the way down to her car, opening the door for her. "Sorry about that. He gets really grumpy sometimes, and I'm not his favorite person." He grinned, looking a little sheepish. "I was a tough kid."

"That's okay, I understand." Cora didn't come from an average family, but she'd seen and heard plenty of parents and their kids interact. She'd seen the oil and water type of relationship she was guessing those two had.

"Thanks for coming by to bring him food. That's really nice of you."

She smiled. "It's no problem. I like visiting with him. He's been lonely. It'll be good for him to have you here."

Ethan looked at the house and shook his head. "We'll see." He looked back to her and offered a slow, easy smile. "Listen, would you like to grab dinner sometime?"

Cora was surprised to find her stomach did a fluttery little flip. Not quite the full-fledged thing it did when Justin smiled at her, but a heck of a lot more than she'd felt for any of the guys she'd met online.

She couldn't help the smile that spread on her face. "I'd like that." She pulled her phone out of her purse. "What's your phone number?"

"You sure you're going to call me if I don't get your number?" he asked and she wasn't entirely sure he wasn't joking. He had to get that women didn't want to give their numbers out right away, right?

His eyes flashed as he gave her a bad boy grin. "Teasing." He rattled off his number and she put it into her phone.

She did know his dad, and his family had lived in Evers for a long time. In fact, it was surprising she hadn't met him before this.

She didn't wait to call him. She sent a text message. "There. Now you have my number."

"Great. I'll call you."

Cora nodded and started the car, waving at him again when he waved at her. He watched as she pulled down the long drive that led to the road.

She could swear she'd heard that when you put yourself

out there and stop looking so hard for The One, you end up meeting more potential Ones. Maybe whoever it was that said that was right. Maybe she'd just met a potential One.

Our heroine smiled as she drove away. Things were beginning to look up.

CHAPTER FIVE

"CORA!" Justin sped to a jog to catch up to Cora.

He came even with her and walked alongside her, their arms brushing. "You just come from work?"

It was a stupid question. It was four-thirty on a school day and she was on the route between the school and her house. She had her bag slung over her shoulder and she was in what she called her school clothes; comfortable business casual loose enough to sit on the floor with the kids if she needed to, but neat enough that she didn't look unprofessional.

Justin's office looked out onto the main street in the center of Evers. He often saw Cora on her way home from school, and if he timed his coffee runs right, he could walk with her for the two blocks to the diner before she turned off to her street.

Lately, it seemed like his chair automatically turned toward the window to watch for her.

She shot him a funny look, but answered. "Yep. On my way home."

"I'm going for coffee," he said. Wow, he was an idiot.

"So, uh, I wanted to see if you wanted to come by the office Saturday to start looking at grants?"

"Can't." She slung her purse higher on her shoulder. "Julia and I are both picking up overtime pay at the school doing some end-of-year jobs before the school closes up for the summer. We're saving up to go to Austin July Fourth weekend for a makeover weekend. I'll save my time off for that."

"A makeover weekend?"

"Yeah, you know, clothes, haircut, makeup."

He frowned. "I like you the way you are."

She rolled her eyes at him. She seemed to be doing that more and more.

A skinny kid with hair that stuck out on the top and sides of his head like a Q-tip ran up to Cora. He was followed by a tired-looking woman and a younger boy who was probably four or five years old. The woman didn't seem inclined to run the way her son had.

"Miss Walker, wait!" The boy gulped for air like he'd been running. He pushed a sheet of paper into Cora's hands. "My mom signed the permission form for me."

Cora smiled and opened the paper, reading it. "Great, Tommy. I'll get you into the computer lab tomorrow and we'll get you started on your summer project." She glanced up at Justin. "Robotics club."

Justin nodded as the mother and younger child caught up to them. Close up, Justin could see that both kids' clothes were worn. The younger boy had a tear in one sleeve and the knees of his pants looked about ready to give up.

Cora knelt. "Hey, Dylan. Did you have fun doing papier-mâché with Mrs. Winters today?" She looked up to the boys' mother. "The younger kids are working on paper-mâché birdhouses in art class this week. I got to help clean up after." Her grin told the adults of the group how that went.

The boy talked animatedly about his project. When he stopped to take a breath, Cora stood and looked ready to speak again, but a guy in jeans and a battered khaki jacket came out of a nearby store.

He only glanced at Justin and the kids and their mother before greeting Cora. "Hey, Cora."

"Ethan, hi." The smile Cora gave the guy set Justin on edge. "Do you know Justin Kensington? And this is Alice Burke and her boys, Tommy and Dylan. Alice and I went to school together and now Tommy is in my classroom."

She hadn't introduced Justin to the woman and her kids.

Ethan gave them all a smile and a nod before turning back to Cora. "Did you get my text? Are we on for dinner? There's a great new sushi place I've been wanting to try."

"Oh, um..."

Justin kept his face straight, but he was grinning on the inside. Poor sucker didn't know Cora hated sushi. Good. Now she could tell him, no.

Justin was coming to terms with the fact that Cora was dating. Hell, he'd be an asshole not to wish her the best, since he couldn't offer her anything more than friendship, but this guy was clearly a jerk.

He tilted his head. Ethan didn't strike Justin as the sushi type. He looked like a beer and pizza kind of guy. Maybe he was just trying to impress Cora.

Cora wasn't the type of woman to be impressed by that kind of thing. She was impressed by people who volun-teered their time to others, not by what someone wore or whether they would bring her to a restaurant with the latest reviews or the hottest new location.

Justin should know. He'd thought for years about what it would take to make Cora happy. He'd had a million ideas over the years of little things she might like. How she would react if he bought the cool robotics set he'd seen for her classroom or what she would say if he showed up one day with a picnic they could share on a hike.

"They have other food, too, though. Tempura and stuff, if you want." Ethan was pressing his hands together in a begging motion.

Justin thought he looked like an idiot, but Cora fell for it.

"Okay, that sounds good," she said. "I still have to do a little work when I get home but I can be ready by about six?"

"Hey, Miss Walker," the younger boy, Dylan, said as he tugged on the hem of Cora's blouse. "Why can't an elephant blow his nose?"

There was an audible groan from Tommy, but Cora gave her full attention to Dylan. "I don't know, Dylan. Why can't an elephant blow his nose?"

"Because elephants are gray!" The little boy cracked up at his punch line, holding his stomach as he did.

Cora offered her hand for a high five. "Good one."

"That makes no sense," Justin said. "A joke is supposed—"

Ethan cut him off, offering his own hand for a high-five from the boy. "You're funny."

Justin kept his mouth shut. He'd never understood why people lied to make kids feel good about themselves. Why didn't they just explain what a joke was and teach him how to tell one?

Alice ruffled Dylan's hair and put her other arm around Tommy's shoulders. "We've got to go. I have to be back at work in ten minutes. It was good to see you, Cora."

The group waved goodbye and walked away.

"So, I'll pick you up at six, Cora?"

Justin had to struggle to keep from growling at Ethan.

Cora glanced Justin's way, pushing her hair behind one ear. "Um, yeah, I'll see you then."

Ethan started walking back toward the store he'd come from. "Perfect."

"That guy? Really?" Justin couldn't help himself. Ethan was all wrong for her.

Cora gave him a sidelong look.

He raised his hands. "I can help, you know."

"Help with what?"

"Finding someone better than Lice Man and Sushi Guy back there."

Again with the eye rolling.

"I'm just saying, you can do better. He should be taller than that guy, and someone who likes learning as much as you do." Justin gave it some thought as they walked along.

She laughed. "Someone who likes learning? Maybe I'll add that to my online profile."

"There are a lot of people right here in Evers. Why go online? What about Tom Casick? He's a great guy, and he's got to be smart. He's an engineer, I think."

"He's studying to be an architect. And he's smart and a great guy—" her patient tone said she was about to explain why he was an idiot again— "but he's also ten years younger than me and he's living in his mother's basement while he takes a year off school to earn money."

"That's a good thing." Justin was warming up to the idea of this. "Instead of getting himself into debt, he's saving money. He won't come out of school with a ton of loans to pay. Smart guy."

They stopped at the corner where she would turn off and he would keep going to the coffee shop.

He looked at her. "Okay, so no-go on Tom Casick?" He thought for a minute. "Pete Sadowski?"

She was already shaking her head. "Dated him in high school."

"Rekindle an old flame?"

She was shaking her head again, but now she had a half smile that said she was a little amused.

"I like Ethan," Cora said gently. "I'm going to dinner with him tonight."

Justin nodded. Right. Sushi Guy it was.

CHAPTER SIX

CORA WATCHED JUSTIN WALK AWAY, then kept going toward her house. She was a block behind Alice and the boys. They were stopped as one of the boys looked to be trying to get a rock or something out of his shoe. She thought about catching up, but didn't. Alice and she had been friends in high school, but when Cora went to college, Alice had stayed here and met her husband, Tyson Burke.

Cora had reached out a few times to Alice, but they'd just been at different points in their lives. Alice was juggling kids and a family and Cora was still trying to find her match.

Cora turned into the library parking lot and cut across toward the back doors of the building.

Ashley's face lit up when she saw Cora push open the door. Cora was younger than Ashley, but she'd been adopted by the Walkers first. When Ashley came into their home, Cora had been a bit like a puppy, always trying to get Ashley to play with her. Ashley hadn't been remotely interested in having a sister. It took time, but now, the sisters were probably closer than they would have been if they'd been biological siblings.

"Hey," Ashley said, leaning on the circulation desk. "You headed home?"

"Yes, as a matter of fact. I have to get dressed." She grinned. "As it turns out, I have a date tonight."

"Nice! Not Lice Man?"

"No. I think he was embarrassed. He blocked me on MatchMeUp and hasn't called."

Ashley frowned. "No big loss. You'll find someone better."

"Ethan Knight asked me out."

Ashley's brows rose. "Wow, talk about taking the plunge. Going right for the bad boy, huh?"

Cora laughed. "I don't really remember him from back then, but I do remember the legend that trailed him at school. He was infamous."

Ashley frowned. "You do get that he was more than just a trouble maker? I mean, I got into trouble, but he took things a hell of a lot further than me."

Cora squirmed. "Well, like, what? What kind of stuff was he into? Drugs and stuff?"

Ashley shook her head, a slow movement that showed she was thinking. "I don't know about drugs, but he drank and I know he and Derrick Ayers stole a car more than once to race it. I think he was into gambling and stuff."

"Well, he must have gotten past all that. He moved home to take care of his dad, and look at you. If we judged you by what you were like in high school..."

She didn't finish the sentence because Ashley had raised her hands up, palms to Cora. "Hey, I wasn't saying he isn't a great guy now. You know me. I think everyone deserves a shot."

Cora hesitated.

Ashley reached out to touch her sister's arm. "Hey, really, I'm sorry. I didn't mean to come down on him. I'm sure he's a great guy now."

"I met him at his dad's house. Ron Knight has been really sick lately and I've been taking muffins and lunch to him sometimes."

Ashley nodded. "I know. Haddie mentioned it. He's the one who says Caufield's Furniture company poisoned his well, right?"

Haddie was Ashley's best friend and co-troublemaker. She was some forty or fifty years older than Ashley, but the two were as close as if they'd been born on the same day and raised together.

"Yes. I don't know all the details of his illness, but he said there's no treatment for it."

"I heard his case is very weak, but I'm not sure if that's just what people want to believe or if it's true. It has to do with trying to prove the chemicals got into the well because of Caufield instead of in some other way."

Cora shook her head. "I have no idea what the case will involve, but I can tell you, he's really sick. He's getting weaker by the day."

Ashley made a show of putting on a smile. "Okay, enough of that. It's sad. Tell me about your date with his son."

Cora grinned. "Dinner tonight. We're going to a Japanese place."

"You hate Japanese."

"No I don't. I hate sushi. I'm sure there's something I'll like that doesn't involve raw fish and seaweed."

"Is he hot?"

Cora tilted her head. "I'm not sure I'd say hot. He's cute. Good looking."

"Why don't I know him? I know everyone in town."

"I'm pretty sure that's not true." Cora said it, but she might be wrong. If anyone could get close to claiming to know everyone in town, it was Ashley. She was the town librarian but she was also a busybody who made it her business to know everyone else's business.

"He just moved back to town to help his dad. He had to close his business to do it, but I think Mr. Knight is really glad he did. I mean, he griped about it, but it's got to be good to have family nearby when you're that sick."

"Oh," Ashley tilted her head. "That's sweet. Ethan gets points for moving home."

"I know, right?"

"What are you gonna wear?"

Cora sighed. "I have no idea. Julia and I are officially saving up for a makeover weekend in Austin over the fourth, but until then, I have to make do with what's in my closet."

"Does any of it not scream *elementary school teacher*?"

"Maybe."

Ashley gave her a look.

"Okay, probably not." Cora waved a hand. "I'll dig around in the back of my closet. There must be something there."

Ashley waved at a group of women walking in the front door of the library. "I have to run. The coupon clippers are here."

The library hosted what seemed like an endless stream of meetings in its back rooms. One of the most faithful was the coupon clippers. Each week, they got together and clipped coupons and compared their savings from the week before.

Ashley leaned over the desk and hugged Cora. "I want all the details when you get home."

Cora walked away, doing her best not to skip and jump like a kid. She just hoped there were good details to tell Ashley later.

CHAPTER SEVEN

"THANK YOU," Cora murmured as Ethan pushed in her chair at the restaurant.

"You're welcome," he said, leaning over closer to her as he spoke.

The hostess waited for him to take his seat before handing him his menu and then left the table. Once they'd ordered their food and handed over their menus, Ethan looked at her across the table.

"I'm glad you could make it tonight. I wasn't sure if you'd want to come out on a school night," he said, his grin telling her he enjoyed the insinuation that they were sneaking out.

"I think if I went out late every weeknight, I'd be too tired to tackle the kids most days, but once or twice a week isn't too bad. Honestly, though, a lot of days, I'm ready to drop into bed at eight o'clock. The kids kind of run me ragged."

"Do you have heavier and lighter times of the year, or is it all pretty even for a first-grade teacher? I mean, I guess it's not like you have heavy exam times or anything, right?"

She shook her head. "No major exams, but at this age, we have assessments we do quarterly and those can be pretty time consuming. There are also parent-teacher conferences. The prep leading up to those, as well as the actual days when they're going on, can be long. Most of the time, though, I spend my afternoons and sometimes evenings writing lesson plans, grading work, adjusting lesson plans, and doing things like individual assessment plans."

"I guess I just tend to think of the time you're in school."

"Hmm," she murmured as she put down her drink. She hated this part of a date. The idle small talk. "It's not like daycare where you show up at a certain time and get a paycheck. There's a lot of behind-the-scenes work that goes into it."

He seemed like he was struggling for something to say, so Cora decided to take over on the questions.

"So, what were you doing in town today?" He'd been coming out of Jansen's Feed Store when they'd set up the date.

He coughed a little, then took a sip of his soda. "Oh, uh, I just picked up a little work there while I get my promo business going here. With the move and all, I lost some of my customers and had to pass some jobs I had committed to off to other people to handle. I used to work summers at Jansen's so he's always happy to give me work."

"Oh yeah, that makes sense."

Ethan shrugged. "He's not bad to work for. It's just a few hours so it doesn't cut into my other stuff. Do you have something you do for work over the summer, or do you just take the summer off?"

Cora swallowed the sip of club soda she'd just taken. "I

wish I made enough during the school year to take the summer off. I always need to take on a part time job."

"What kinds of things have you done in the past?"

"I've worked at the book store, an art supply shop a few towns over, and as an online teacher for a homeschooling summer program."

"And this year?"

"I'll be doing some tutoring and teaching a summer robotics class for some of the school kids."

They were quiet while the waiter brought out their meals. When he'd walked away, Ethan picked up the thread of the conversation. "Robotics?"

Cora nodded. "It's kind of cool. By the end of the summer, I'll break the kids into teams and they get to build a robot and we have a battle royale."

Ethan laughed. "Sounds bloody."

"Figuratively speaking, only, thank goodness. But, yes, there are robot casualties." Cora focused on cutting her Teriyaki Chicken trying to think of a question to keep the conversation going.

She went with the work angle again, this time turning it toward him. "It was really good that you were able to move your business here. I'm sure your dad appreciates having you back at the ranch."

Ethan's face fell. "I need to try to help him."

Cora was an idiot. She shouldn't have brought up the issue of his father's condition. Before she could pull back from the topic, Ethan went on.

"My dad started selling off pieces of our land a long time ago. My mom and him only had a chance to have me before she died, and I guess running a ranch without a ton of sons around as free labor is tough."

"I'm sorry about your mom," Cora said. "Were you young when she died?"

He nodded. "I was four. I don't remember much about her."

He'd been younger than Cora was when her mom had left her. She never knew her dad and wasn't even sure her mom had ever told him she was pregnant. There'd been no name on her birth certificate, so the state hadn't had any way to know who he was, much less contact him.

"It must be hard watching your dad sell pieces of the land. It's been in your family for a long time?" Cora was making a guess. Many of the ranches in the area were passed down from generation to generation.

Ethan shook his head. "I never minded, and I don't honestly think he did. Neither of us liked the ranching life. I guess it's too bad we didn't figure that out earlier and do something else with the land." He looked up at her. "My dad loved me, though. I always knew that. He did the best he could."

It broke Cora's heart that he had come home for what would probably be the end of his father's life.

"I just want to be there for him now. I need to do all I can to make this right for him. I'm hoping to convince my dad to move into town. I can get us an apartment." He looked up from his food. "It has to be a good idea to get him away from the soil and the well as long as those chemicals are still out there, you know?"

Cora's brows drew together. "He's using bottled water, though, right?"

"Yeah, but I figure it can't hurt to get him out of there. He's not sure he wants to leave the house, though. He's lived there all his life."

"It must be hard on him." Cora wiped her mouth and put her napkin back in her lap. "And on you."

Cora didn't have to think twice about whether she would do that for her parents. They had adopted her when she had no one. They'd given her unconditional love, siblings, a home. They'd given her a place to belong.

She searched for a way to pull him back from the hard topic of his father's condition.

"So, um, do you like to read?" She almost cringed at the question. It was so first-dateish.

Ethan pushed his plate back. "I don't read much. I watch movies. I have an old car I like to work on." He grinned. "I read manuals and car magazines."

"What kind of movies do you like?"

"Action movies, sci-fi."

"Do superhero movies fall in there somewhere?"

His smile was slow. He was leaning back in his chair now, and she could see heat in his eyes as he watched her. She had that jittery first date feeling in the pit of her stomach, but it was a good kind of jittery.

"Sure. Superhero movies count."

Cora raised a hand as if swearing an oath. "I swear. I love super hero movies. And I know it's probably sacrilege to say it, but I don't care if it's Marvel Comics or whatever that other one is. I love them equally."

That brought laughter from him but there was definitely an edge of incredulity to his expression. "That *other one* is DC Comics and it's clearly superior. It's Justice League. How can you not see the supremacy?"

She waved a hand. "I'm an equal-opportunity viewer."

He egged her on. "All right, we need to have a Justice League marathon so I can convince you to come over to the right side of the light."

"You're on. As long as there's popcorn and ice cream, I'm there."

Cora's nerves were beginning to wane as they talked. Ethan was nice. He didn't give her the full-on butterflies doing jumping jacks and setting off fireworks in the stomach thing that Justin did, but he was good looking in his own way. She liked his crooked smile and the way he seemed to stick by his dad even though the two seemed to fight like cats and dogs. Or like father and son, she supposed.

Their conversation went to town gossip and updating Ethan on the major developments he'd missed in town over the past five years when he'd been living in San Marcos.

"It's still hard to believe your sister married the Chief of Police." Ethan shook his head. "I was a senior when she was a freshman in high school, but I could tell even then she was going to keep Sheriff Bowden busy."

Sheriff Bowden had been sheriff in the town when she and Cora were in school. He'd brought Ashley home more than once when she got into trouble.

Ethan must have noticed her expression because he rushed to smooth over her sister's past. "She wasn't too bad. From what I've heard, she only caused a little innocent trouble here and there. After what I'd put him through, she was probably a walk in the park."

Ashley had been brought home in the Sheriff's custody when she scaled the town's water tower and got stuck, and another time when she'd spray painted the windows in the principal's office. There'd been one time, though, that she'd been caught drinking. That had sent their parents over the edge.

Cora cleared her throat. "What kind of trouble did you cause?"

Ethan's brows rose. "You didn't hear stories about me?"

She flushed. "I heard a few."

Ethan reached across the table to run his finger lazily over her hand. "Nothing major. Just kid stuff."

Cora wasn't sure that was true. She'd heard he once stole a car and ended up driving it off the road into a field. Another story said he'd been arrested at a raid on an illegal gambling house, but he'd been let off with community service because he was a minor. She didn't know which stories were true.

They passed on dessert and Ethan paid the bill.

As they walked back to his car, he told her more about his plans to expand and build a website to sell promotional goods instead of opening another storefront. Less overhead meant a more stable business and he could stay in town as long as his dad needed him.

When he dropped her off at her house, would he kiss her goodnight? She hated the fact she was obsessing over that question. He was talking as they walked to the car, but she'd gotten so focused on whether he would kiss her good-night, she'd lost track of what he was saying.

Then he was opening the car door for her and she slipped into the seat, letting him shut the door for her.

He came around to his side and sat, looking across at her before he started the car. "I'm glad we did this tonight."

Cora bit her lip, but then smiled. "Me, too. I had a really good time tonight."

It was true, she realized.

He leaned across the car and slid one hand around the back of her neck, pulling her toward him. His mouth was soft and gentle on hers. She kissed him back, tilting her head when he deepened the kiss.

He stopped before long, and she let her eyes fall to her lap. The kiss had been nice. The perfect length. Not too intense but just right for a first date. And she liked that she didn't have to spend the whole car ride home wondering if he'd kiss her goodnight.

It was like that scene in *Good Will Hunting* where they decide to get the kiss out of the way before the end of the date.

"I've been wanting to do that from the minute I walked into my dad's kitchen and saw you there," Ethan said.

Cora flushed, her eyes shooting to meet his gaze. "Really?"

"Really," he said, his crooked smile was broad as he started the car and pulled out of the spot.

And, yes, he kissed her goodnight again on her front steps.

CHAPTER EIGHT

"SO?"

Cora looked up from her lunch to see Julia standing in her doorway. Her friend held out a cookie wrapped in a napkin.

Cora took the cookie and waited for Julia to sink into the chair next to her desk that was usually reserved for students who needed a little extra focus.

"Tell me about date two."

Cora leaned in. It was more exciting talking about dating now that she was doing more than surfing the web and sending messages back and forth to guys who looked like they might be a good match. She and Ethan had gone on a second date over the weekend and he asked her if she could have dinner sometime during the week, too.

"We went to a movie Saturday night and he held my hand through the whole movie."

"Did you make out?" Julia looked over her shoulder as she asked the question, as though checking for random students who might come into the room. They didn't have a whole lot of time free for lunch.

"A little." Cora could feel her cheeks heat. "We went for a walk after the movie and got ice cream cones."

"Awww, so sweet."

"It was kind of romantic."

Julia's smile told Cora she agreed. "So, you like him?"

"I do. I feel comfortable with him. It's like being with my brothers, except not."

That got Julia to sit up. "That's not exactly a good thing."

Cora waved her hand. "No, no, I don't mean it that way. I just mean that he's comfortable to be with. On our first date, there was a little bit of awkwardness, and I think I was kind of intimidated by the fact that he was kind of a bad boy in high school, but he's nice now."

"Nice?" Julia raised a brow.

"Yes, nice." Cora squirmed a little.

"You realize a guy should make your toes curl." Julia gave her a meaningful look. "I mean really curl. Like when he kisses you, your heart should flip over and you should feel his kiss all the way to your toes."

"Yeah, I'm getting the toes thing. You've mentioned toes several times," Cora said, feeling a little grumpy.

She'd love to have a guy affect her that way, but she wasn't living in her sister's romance novels. She wasn't going to hope that somehow, she and Justin would miraculously happen.

Cora wanted a real-life boyfriend that might someday lead to a real-life marriage and real-life children of her own.

Ethan was a real-life kind of guy. He was what she wanted, even if the flip in her stomach when he kissed her had been small, and she'd maybe only felt that kiss in her belly and nowhere near her toes. Or even her knees.

"Toes are important," Julia said primly. "Are you still checking your online profile to keep your options open?"

Cora chewed on her lip. "Well, I haven't been. It seems kind of wrong to be dating someone and still checking my profile for other guys."

Julia stood. "We better get up to our kids." She pointed to Cora, though, as they left the classroom. "But, I'm telling you. You need to keep your options open. Until you guys say it's exclusive, you need to keep looking for Mr. Toe Curler."

CHAPTER NINE

WORKING with Justin on the grants might have been a mistake. Being around him was a stupid idea.

She had seen the temptation coming. She wasn't an idiot.

What she didn't see coming was that he would try to help her with her love life. They'd spent the morning looking through the grants he'd pulled from a database and talking about which application they'd file.

Then he'd raised the issue of dating. All she could think was how ironic it was that he was finally talking to her about a date, and it was to set her up with someone else. That wasn't what she'd envisioned all these years of pining for him.

She flinched. She hated thinking that she'd spent years waiting for him to ask her out. Why hadn't she seen reality sooner?

"You want to set me up with your friend?" She really thought he would drop this.

"I think you'll really like him. He's a great guy. He runs one of the organizations we fund over in Bandera."

"Isn't that over an hour away?" It was all Cora could think to say.

How could she tell him that it hurt like hell to have him trying to set her up with someone else? It didn't matter that she was already dating other people. What mattered was that she wasn't ready to talk to Justin about other guys. They were friends, but she wasn't ready for that kind of friendship. Apparently, it didn't bother him at all.

Justin shrugged. "Your sister and Garrett made the long-distance thing work."

Cora nodded. "Yeah, well, thanks, but I'm gonna pass."

"Are you still seeing Ethan?"

"I like him. He said he'd call again."

"And you'll say yes when he does?"

A knock on the door interrupted them before she could answer.

"Yes," Justin called out.

His assistant, Amanda, entered. "Justin, I have the report from the Boston charity. You asked me to get it to you when the numbers came in."

Justin reached for the file Amanda handed him. "Did they hit their goals?"

"No. They're short by eight percent on mission spending."

Cora waited as Justin read the report. She wasn't sure if she should stay or go wait in the lobby until he was finished.

Justin answered her question when he looked up at her. "Since Raise the Veil's two main goals are to spread the word that being the victim of domestic violence is nothing to be ashamed about and to help fund organizations that are serving victims of violence and abuse on the ground, we have strict requirements each funded organization has to meet."

"What kind of requirements?" Cora asked. She knew a lot about what the organization did through her friendship with Laura, but she didn't know the details of their programming and funding.

"We look for organizations in regions where we feel the need is greatest. That's determined based on reported domestic violence, estimated underreported domestic violence, funding going to the area, and a few other factors. Once we do that, we identify a charity to serve that region. The charity needs to hit certain percentages of funding going directly to mission spending, administration, and other funding. Since we provide a large portion of the chosen charity's funding goals, we have stricter requirements than some charitable accreditation organizations require."

Cora nodded. It all made sense and would help Raise the Veil be sure their funding was getting through to the people they were trying to serve.

Justin continued. "We require a minimum of seventy percent of the funding the organization takes in from us and from other sources go to mission goals. We allow twenty-two percent to go to administrative costs, and the rest can go to soliciting funding from other sources."

"And they've missed that?" She looked from Justin to Amanda and back.

"Twice," Amanda said. "We had a volunteer go and help them look at ways to revamp their spending to meet the goals. They were able to make the targets for six months, then they slipped again last month."

"And now this month," Justin said, frowning at the papers in his hand again. He looked back to Amanda. "We have an alternate organization in the area, correct?"

Cora looked at him. He was in his business mode now.

No nonsense, ready to make whatever decisions had to be made. He could have been running a Fortune 500 company. As it was, she knew he did a lot to manage his family's wealth. His mother was still alive and active in that as well, but she knew Justin met with his mom regularly to help make decisions about investments and things.

She wondered if it bothered him that he didn't have children. His brother was Laura's child's biological father, so his blood was continuing down the line in that way, but the Kensington family had once been a large family with branches growing thick and strong on the family tree. Now, it was down to his mom, him, and Laura's daughter, Jamie.

Amanda's answer pulled Cora's attention back to the conversation. "Yes. There's a group that applied for funding from us two years ago, but we were already committed in the region. I've kept tabs on their numbers and it looks like they can meet our requirements."

Justin nodded. "Pull it."

Cora's brows went up but she didn't say anything.

Amanda slipped out of the room and Justin turned to Cora.

"You don't agree?" he asked.

"With your decision?" She looked toward the door, as though she might see the reasoning of his decision laid out for her in the space his assistant had recently occupied. "No, I don't necessarily disagree. It must just be hard to know you're likely about to shut that group down. Whoever was getting services from them will be left without the resources they were expecting. The employees may very well be cut, if the place doesn't close altogether with the loss of such a huge portion of their funding in one blow."

He nodded, but she could see he wouldn't change his mind. "The people they were serving will head over to the alternative group and with our funding, they'll be able to take them on. They'll do a better job of meeting the community's needs because they're putting more money into mission goals than the first group. The transition won't be great, but the long-term outlook is better."

"You're really in the right place, you know that?"

Justin leaned back in his chair, watching her like he didn't trust what she was about to say. "What do you mean?"

"You're really doing what you should be doing. I don't think a lot of people would be able to make the kind of tough decisions this role demands, and be able to still be compassionate and not jaded. You've really made this organization into something important and meaningful."

Justin just looked back at her, eyes guarded like he wasn't fully able to believe what she was saying. Cora didn't drop her gaze. If they were going to do this friendship thing, she would do it wholeheartedly. That meant helping him to see what he meant to the people he was trying to serve. Because she had a feeling Justin didn't see himself at all the same way others saw him. She had a feeling the abuse and violence that had taken place in his home had shaped him and affected him in ways he couldn't bring himself to see; in ways he couldn't even understand yet, much less address.

CHAPTER TEN

"LAURA TELLS me you're not going to fight for Cora."

Justin dropped the contract he'd been reading and looked up at his mother's words. He was no idiot. When his mother walked into his office unannounced and made a statement like that, it meant she planned to lecture him. He wasn't going to get a damned thing done until she'd said all she planned to say. The faster he let her get it out, the faster he'd get her out of his office so he could get back to work.

He dropped into his chair and watched as his mother settled into the chair across from him. There was a time Martha Kensington wouldn't have been caught dead in anything other than full makeup, hair, and a thousand-dollar suit. Now, she sat in front of him in jeans and a T-shirt that said "Professional Grandma at Work ... Stand Back."

There was also a time when he and his mother were barely on speaking terms. Even when they had talked, he wouldn't describe their relationship as loving. Justin hadn't grown up in a family where parents hugged and kissed the kids or said words like, *I love you.* He'd grown up in a house where outward appearances were what mattered. His mother had been a person he didn't very much like.

The woman in front of him was different. Not a wholly new person, but she was changing. In the past three years, she'd done a lot to make up for the things she'd said and done in the past.

She looked at him as though she expected a response and he had to replay her words in his head to try to catch up to her. She'd said something about fighting for Cora.

"What are you talking about?" he asked.

"Cora Walker has decided to date. Everyone knows it," she said, as if she had to explain that. In Evers, you didn't have to explain much of anything to anyone. News flew around town like wildfire almost before it happened. "Laura said you're not going to fight for her."

"Mom, there's nothing to fight for. Cora and I are friends." He picked up the contract and began skimming the pages again.

He could see his mother out of the corner of his eye. She couldn't completely hide her past persona. She sat stiffly in her chair, back ramrod straight as though she could fend off the world if she held herself just so. She'd spent a lot of years that way, cutting herself off from feeling anything.

When Justin's brother Patrick died and it came out that he'd been abusing Laura, Justin and his mother had said things to each other that could never be taken back. He'd known his mother had been aware of the abuse Laura suffered and she'd done nothing to help. In fact, she'd helped to cover it up. The fact Laura and his mother had a relationship now was something that floored him.

He and his mother were closer than they'd ever been, but that didn't mean there wasn't still a lot they had never dealt with. The issues they'd never addressed could fill all of

Texas and half the surrounding states. They'd left the world they had once inhabited behind, for the most part, but there would always be a wall between them that he didn't think they could knock down.

She surprised him when she pressed on. It wasn't like her to talk about personal issues with him, but she didn't drop this the way he thought she would. "Laura has a theory about your feelings for Cora and why you haven't acted on them."

He knew exactly what Laura's theory about him and Cora was, and he didn't want to discuss it with his mom.

"I have to tell you, I think Laura is right. She's pretty intuitive when it comes to this kind of thing."

Laura was caring and loving and giving. All the things their family wasn't. He'd always thought it was a miracle Patrick had been able to get her to marry him.

Justin went back to the start of the page and tried reading it again. He wasn't absorbing much of it, despite the fact his eyes were traveling over the words.

His family had never been one for hugs and kisses and soft words. His dad had talked at his brother and him, more than with them. They'd been taught about the expectations of the family and groomed to meet those standards. If his parents had said "I love you" to him more than once or twice in their lives before this past few years, he didn't remember it.

"Justin." His mother's voice was almost a whisper. "Please."

He looked up and froze at the look on his mother's face. She was uncomfortable. He could see it. She didn't want to talk about this any more than he did. But more than that, he could see determination in her eyes.

She looked down for a minute before meeting his eyes.

"Don't interrupt me because I need to get this out and I don't know if I can say this more than once."

Justin nodded, waiting.

"What you and Laura have done with this place is amazing. Every day, you're helping to reach out and teach people about abuse. You're helping to get women out of situations they can't get out of easily. You're teaching women that reaching out for help shouldn't bring shame or embarrassment. I couldn't be prouder of the work you're doing here."

Justin opened his mouth to say something—he wasn't sure what, but something. His mother leveled him with a look.

"The thing is, Justin, I don't think you're learning the lessons you need to be learning here. You need to forgive yourself for what you see as your failures in what happened Laura and me."

Justin felt a painful lump swell and clog his throat. It seemed like it might cut off his air. His mother had never confirmed what he feared. That his father had hit her the way his brother hit Laura. He and Laura had talked a lot about what she went through, but with his mother, it was the kind of thing they all knew happened, but they'd silently agreed not to go there.

She talked now, and it seemed as though each word cost her. He knew talking about what she'd been through was crucial, but it killed him to hear it.

"Your father wasn't like Patrick was with Laura. I've talked to her and I know she went through hell with Patrick. She was living with violence every day. Your brother was sick, Justin, and by the time I realized it, I had walled myself off in a cell of alcohol and pills."

She seemed to go to another place as she spoke. "Your

father wasn't violent in the same way Patrick was. I thought your father loved me. I loved him with all my naïve heart when we were first married."

She took a steadying breath. "When he hit me the first time, I started the cycle of making excuses for him, of blaming myself for not being perfect, not being what he needed. I don't need to tell you about that part. Your work here has taught you what can happen to a woman in that position. There was so much shame. It never occurred to me that it was your father's fault, that maybe he'd been taught by his father to handle things that way. It never dawned on me that I had any choice other than to cover it up and hide my shame from the world."

Justin felt the rage he had for his father swell inside him. It ate at his chest, clawing into him with such force it was physically painful. But alongside the rage for his father was more anger and hatred for himself. He'd let this happen. He hadn't seen what his mother was going through. What kind of son doesn't see this?

In his work at Raise the Veil, he'd read accounts of sons growing to the point where they were able to fight back and protect their mothers. Justin had never once done that. He'd never even known his mother had been abused. She hadn't walked around with black eyes and bruises, but he could think back now and catalogue her injuries. Catalogue all the times he'd let her down.

He remembered a day when she'd had a large bruise on the side of her face. It didn't look like a punch, so his child mind had no trouble believing her when she said she walked into the edge of the door when she got up in the middle of the night for something and didn't turn on the lights.

She'd broken her wrist twice, but there had been good

reasons for both incidents. Over the past few years, he'd relived every little scratch or bruise, and every story she'd concocted for each of them.

How had he never heard the fights? How had he not heard her crying?

"Your father didn't hit me often. He saw it as a lack of control when he did and he never liked to be out of control. The thing was, he blamed every slip in control on me. Your father's words were always more painful than his punches. If he lost his temper, it was because I had pushed him too far, because I had failed. I wasn't good enough to be a Kensington. So, I tried harder. I made myself into the perfect Kensington matriarch. I put on the mask and showed the world, showed all of you, what was expected. And when I saw the same thing happening to Laura, I wasn't strong enough to get her out of there. I was angry and bitter and thought the world owed me something for what I had gone through. I told her to suck it up and put on the face the world expected to see. I tried to turn her into me."

His mother was very still. "I think on some level, I wanted someone to go through what I'd been through. I know that's sick, but I think I felt like I shouldn't have to suffer that alone."

There was a long, painful silence and he was sure his mother was doing everything in her power not to cry. It was written on her face. When she spoke, the ache and pain carried in her voice. "It is my greatest shame."

Justin felt his throat constrict and he wasn't sure that he'd be able to breathe in a minute.

His mother cleared her throat, her face etched with determination as if she could barrel through this. "You didn't see what was going on because I didn't let you. Patrick knew, but by the time he figured it out, your father had already warped him so much. I realized he would get hold of you soon and change who you were. That's when I sent you away to school. I wanted you away from your father, and away from Patrick. I drove a wedge between all of you so that he couldn't poison you. *I* did all of that, Justin. You're not to blame for not seeing what was going on. I was very good at hiding it, so there's nothing here for you to pay penance for. There's nothing for you to be punished for. There's no reason that you shouldn't grab life with all you're worth and live it. Find love. Find happiness. You deserve that more than any of us."

She stood, then, looking down at where he still sat. He should say something. He should reach out and hug her. He should tell her it's all right. He didn't.

She paused in front of his desk. "What Laura and I went through was horrible, and I'm glad we're out of it, but I think you need to realize we weren't the only victims of it."

Justin knew all of that intellectually. He knew the victims of domestic abuse included those who lived around it and witnessed it. Knowing that intellectually was very different than being able to accept it in his heart.

"I want you to let yourself live and love. You are nothing like your brother or your father. You could never hurt a woman the way they did. It's just not in you." She put her hand on his. "Your heart is too strong for that. It's why I sent you away all those years ago. I sent you away because I knew you would never keep that secret if you discovered it. You would have stood up to your father for me, and at the time, he was much too powerful and strong for you. He would have hurt you and I couldn't stand that. I could numb a lot with alcohol and pills, but I couldn't numb the pain I would have felt if your father turned on you."

She looked fierce when she said the next words. "It's

one thing to break the cycle of abuse. I know you can do that. But you also need to be sure the abuse doesn't haunt you forever and strip your life of what it should be."

He sat frozen, processing what she'd said as she left the room. It was a long time before he could speak, and even then, what came out was a harsh, grating whisper. "I'm so sorry, mom. I'm so damned sorry."

Two days later, Justin still felt wrung-out from the talk with his mother. He had gone home, taking the rest of the day off. He'd been in no shape to work or see anyone. His mom was right. He hadn't fully dealt with any of what his family had been through.

Now he sat at his desk, wondering where this all left him. Yes, his mother was right. Yes, he'd been punishing himself for the wrongs he believed he'd committed, the failures he had taken on as his own, even though, if anything they belonged only to a young boy who couldn't have known any better.

But that didn't mean he could run right out and change. It was hard to move on from what you thought you needed to do and be for so many years. He'd thought he couldn't have happiness and love. That he didn't deserve it. Shaking off that feeling wasn't going to come overnight.

Besides, Justin thought, as he watched the scene unfolding out his office window. Cora was walking down the front path of the building to a waiting Ethan. She was happy. She was with Ethan, and she was happy. She'd made it clear that Ethan was who she wanted. Justin wouldn't do anything to disrupt that now.

His phone rang and he turned to lift the receiver to his ear.

"Justin Kensington," he said into the phone, still watching the spot where Cora had been.

"You haven't been to a Sunday dinner in over two months." May Bishop's voice came through the phone without preamble.

May was Laura's new mother-in-law and unofficial matriarch of the town. Almost everyone in town had been ordered to come to Sunday dinner at one time or another. Justin was on the list of people who were expected to make an appearance more routinely than not. He'd failed at that lately.

"Sorry, May. I've been—"

"Busy," she finished in a tone that said she wasn't buying it. "I'll tell you what. You swing by the ranch this afternoon to have tea with me and I'll forget all about it."

"Uh, tea?"

"Tea," she said, and hung up.

CHAPTER ELEVEN

JUSTIN HAD BEEN RIGHT. He wasn't a tea kind of guy. But he did like May's cookies and he liked May, so he was pretty happy three hours later as he sat in May's living room.

Josh, May's boyfriend, stood after a few minutes of conversation. "I'm going to head out to the greenhouses to see Laura. I'll be back in a bit." Laura had two greenhouses where she ran an organic seed company when she wasn't over at Raise the Veil or speaking at events to spread the word about domestic violence.

Josh's exit was a blatant effort to leave May and Justin alone, and Justin braced himself for whatever was coming.

May watched Josh leave with a smile on her face. She had her hair in the two grey braids she usually wore and the cane she used to get around in the house leaned on her chair.

"I send him out to the greenhouses when I need him out of my hair." There was love in her voice and Justin wondered if she and Josh would someday marry. He had been a friend of her and her husband's but the two hadn't started their relationship until her husband had been gone for years. Josh lived on the ranch with May, so maybe they didn't plan to marry.

"You don't like him out of your hair very often, do you?"

"No," she said, a small smile teasing her lips as she sipped from her tea. "I really don't."

He waited, knowing she had called him here for a reason.

She didn't disappoint. "You know, I'm known for being direct."

"I do."

"And for my sage advice."

He laughed. "Yes, ma'am."

"I've also gotten to be close to your mother over the last year."

Justin sobered. He'd known this was coming, but still, it was hard to talk about.

"She's worried about you," May said. "She told me she's afraid the damage from her relationship with your father is affecting you."

Justin put his tea cup down and sat forward, leaning his elbows on his knees. "She's right," he said, feeling the weight of what he'd been living with ease a little more. It seemed as though that had been happening more and more. The more he talked about what his family had been like, the more it seemed like he was freed from the past.

"But I think," he said, "that it's getting better. I think *I'm* getting better."

"That makes me happy to hear. I think you deserve to find some happiness of your own."

The thought made him sad and he realized it was because he didn't know if it might be too late for that. He'd missed his chance with Cora. Logic told him there would be someone else for him someday, but that wasn't what his heart was telling him.

Hell, when had he become a guy who sat around talking about his heart?

"Well, there's a sad face."

Justin laughed. He could imagine May saying that to one of her boys when they were little. May wasn't at all like his mom had been. She was the kind of woman who would be tough on her boys, expecting a lot from them, but she was also the kind of mom who would have given hugs and kisses out liberally.

"I'm all right. Just coming to terms with some of what I've given up by not dealing with all of this sooner."

She raised a brow. "Oh I don't know about that. It might not be too late. Cora is dating, but she's not married or even engaged yet."

"She's found someone she likes a lot. I'm not going to get in the way of that."

"I'm not saying you should get in the way of anything, but don't count yourself out yet. Work on letting yourself be happy for now. That should be enough to keep you busy for a while anyway. But until she's made up her mind about Ethan, don't go crossing anyone off your list yet."

He nodded. He didn't have a list. Well, maybe he did, but if he did it was a one person list. For right now, the only person he wanted was Cora Walker.

But May was right. Maybe for now he should focus on just living his life since he'd forgiven himself for not doing something to help his mom or Laura. Maybe for now, just living with that weight off of him was enough.

CHAPTER TWELVE

JUSTIN HAD FORCED himself to come to the Kick-Off Chili Festival that started the summer each year in Evers. The summer was as much about beer and friends as it was about chili, but for this day, chili reigned supreme in Evers.

He'd realized after his talk with his mom that she and Laura had been right. He'd been punishing himself for years now. He still wasn't convinced he shouldn't blame himself for not seeing what had been happening to his mom and Laura, but he was beginning to see that he didn't need to pay for that forever. Laura and his mother had started their lives over. They were happy.

And they wanted him to be happy.

"Wow. Buttoned-up Justin Kensington at the chili festival. Imagine my surprise." Cora sat in the empty spot next to him at the picnic table and tapped his plastic beer cup with her cup of lemonade in a toast. "I think I've seen you at more social events this past two weeks than I have in the last six months. You look different, too."

He turned to her with a smile, but had to force that smile to stay in place when he saw Ethan next to her. Ethan slid into the seat on the other side of Cora, nodding a greeting to Justin.

Cora was looking at Justin, her eyes narrowed like she was studying him. He studied her back.

She looked happy, too, he noticed, and he hated that he had a feeling it was Ethan who was making her look that way.

Justin already knew he'd waited too long. Cora had slipped away from him. As much as he liked seeing her happy, it was still going to take a hell of a lot of effort not to act on the urge to tear her away from the asshole.

He nodded at Ethan before moving his gaze back to Cora. She wore her dark hair in a ponytail and her cheeks were flush with pink like she'd been laughing.

"I've heard it's a sin to live in Evers and not make it out to the Chili Festival and the Strawberry Festival," he said by way of an answer. "My mom said she's going to make me a list of the other things I'm not supposed to miss. I'm hoping they're all food focused."

Cora looked at the bowls in front of him. Three were empty but there were still two left. "Are you working your way through all the contest entries?"

At the chili festival, you could get free spoon-sized samples of the entries, or you could buy tickets to be turned in at the booths for full bowls.

Justin held up a string of tickets and patted his still-flat stomach as though it was bloated. "I'm pacing myself."

Cora pointed to the next full one in his lineup. "Everyone knows you save the Hart brothers' entry for last. It's so spicy, it kills your taste buds for the rest of them," she said, shaking her head at him. "You're a real rookie at this."

He only grinned and pulled that one closer. "I like

spicy. If it kills my taste buds for all the others, I'll just go back and get more of that one."

Her parents walked up on the opposite side of the table, chili bowls and a plate of nachos in hand. "Are these seats taken?"

Cora looked to Justin. He waved a hand at the seats with a smile for her parents. "Have at it. My mom is here somewhere with Laura and Jamie. Cade's waiting in line for beer, but there's plenty of room."

Ethan slipped his arm around Cora's shoulders. Justin clenched his fist, then made an effort to release it.

"Okay, mom, what's the deal? You look ready to bounce out of your seat."

Justin looked at Cora's mom. He hadn't noticed it before but she did look happier than usual. Not that she wasn't a happy person. She was. But she had a wide smile on her face and Cora was right. She was all but bouncing in her seat.

Her mom pressed her lips together and shook her head. "I'm just having fun, that's all."

Cora let out a huff that sounded like half laughter, half disbelief. Cora looked to her dad. "What gives?"

He shook his head. "You have to wait for Ashley. She'll be here in a minute. She and Garrett are getting funnel cake."

Cora's mom elbowed Cora's dad. "Make it a little more obvious, why don't you?"

Cora started her own version of bouncing happy. "When? How far along is she? Do they know what they're having?"

Was she saying Ashley was pregnant? Justin looked to Cora's mom for answers, but her mom made a zipping motion over her lips in the standard, "I'm not saying a word" motion.

Tommy Burke ran up to the table before anyone could say anything else. "Miss Walker, I can't find my mom." He glanced around the table at the other adults and Justin could see he was fighting back panic, then back at Cora. "I was supposed to go to the bathroom, then go right back to where she was waiting with Dylan, but I can't find her."

He wasn't in full-on breakdown mode yet, but looked like he might get there if he didn't set eyes on his mom soon.

Cora stood, taking Tommy's hand. "No problem, buddy. We'll find her."

Justin stood. "Do you need help?"

Cora opened her mouth to speak, but Ethan had risen with her, setting a hand on her back. "I'll come."

Ethan grinned at Tommy. "It'll be an adventure. Besides, I've been hoping your brother has some more jokes for me. I could use a laugh, you know."

Tommy kicked the ground. "Mom said your dad is sick and he's gonna die. That means he'll go to Heaven and you don't get to see him anymore." He raised his eyes. "I'm sorry about that."

Ethan kneeled. "Thanks, Tommy. That's nice to hear."

"Are you gonna miss him?"

Ethan's eyes were filled with sorrow, but Justin could see he was attempting to mask the depths of it from the young boy. "I am."

Cora put her hand on Tommy's shoulder. "Let's go find your momma, okay?"

They walked off together, Tommy promising more jokes as soon as they found Dylan.

Cora turned and waved at Justin. When she turned

back, Ethan took her hand and she looked up at him, a smile on her face.

"She's happy, Justin."

Justin pulled his eyes from Cora and Ethan to find Cora's mother watching him.

She repeated herself. "She's happy."

Justin collected his empty bowls and stood, meeting Mrs. Walker's eyes. "I know. I won't do anything to change that."

He tossed the empty bowls in a nearby garbage can and set off across the field in the other direction. He needed to put some distance between himself and Cora Walker. If he didn't, there was no way he could live up to the promise he'd just made to her mother.

CHAPTER THIRTEEN

"THAT WAS A FUN DAY," Ethan said, walking Cora up to her door. "I'd forgotten how much fun some of the town festivals can be."

"Well, you're in for a treat. They've added three new events to the lineup. There's now a big art show at the end of the summer and there are two new winter festivals, too. A snowman competition and a winter carnival."

"A snowman competition?" Ethan looked around as though their location had mysteriously changed. "They know this is Texas, right?"

Cora grinned and opened the door, leading the way into her duplex. "That one, you can blame on my sister. Ashley's on the committee that plans the events. She thought it would be fun to make snow for the kids once a year. It worked out surprisingly well last year. They brought in a snow making machine and made three huge mounds of snow on the town green. The kids all got to climb in it and build snowmen. It's going to be an annual thing now."

She turned to him in the entryway. "Do you want something to drink? We could, um, maybe watch a movie or something."

Ethan shoved his hands in his pockets and nodded. "Sure, that sounds great."

Cora grinned and pointed to the couch. "Why don't you find a movie while I grab drinks and maybe popcorn?"

When she came back in the room and sat next to him, he pulled her closer to him on the couch, wrapping his arms around her. Cora sank in to his side and he started the movie. She should have known. He'd gone for *The Dark Knight Rises*.

"DC Comics, I take it?"

He gave her a mock look of scorn.

Cora laughed and settled back against his shoulder.

Ethan's hand brushed up and down her shoulder as the movie played. They were only twenty minutes into it when he turned her in his arms.

He brought his hand to her chin and tilted her face to his, kissing her. Cora kissed him back, feeling his arms pull her closer to him.

Her eyes drifted shut as his tongue caressed the seam of her lips.

Cora sighed, and opened for him as he took the kiss deeper.

It took only a moment for her to realize she had begun to picture Justin in her mind. She'd somehow begun to imagine it was his hands on her, his mouth taking hers.

She squeaked and opened her eyes, straightening. "You should ... I should ..." She looked over her shoulder, like there might be some excuse in the air hovering for her to pluck it out of the sky.

Ethan looked a little startled, but he recovered quickly, a smile hitting his eyes. "Chicken?" he asked.

"Yes!" She grabbed onto the excuse, even though she had a feeling Ethan took that as a challenge more than anything. She laughed. "Sorry, no. I'm just a little worn out, that's all. Can we do this another time?"

She flinched on the inside but tried to keep a straight face. How do you say, *we can't do this because I can't keep the face of my friend/former obsession out of my mind when you touch me?*

He looked at her as she stood and began gathering their drinks and the popcorn bowl. "I should have gotten to bed earlier last night. I stayed up late reading. It was a good book, though, and you know how it is. One more chapter, right?"

He gave her a quizzical look but stood, taking the popcorn bowl from her and walking it into the kitchen with her.

"I mean one chapter always turns into two and then before you know it, you've read them all and it's three o'clock."

She was babbling. She bit her lip and he leaned over to look her in the eye.

"Get some sleep, Cora."

That was all he said, but there was humor in it. She realized he probably thought she was nervous about having sex with him. He didn't seem concerned. He seemed like he thought it was a given that they would end up in bed.

Damn, that's what she got for dating a bad boy. She was out of her league.

When he'd gone and she shut and locked the door behind him, Cora slid down to the floor and banged her head against her knees, trying to knock some sense into herself. She'd just had a perfectly handsome, perfectly nice real-life man kissing her. There was nothing wrong with him. Not a damned thing. He was ... perfectly perfect.

Except for the fact that he wasn't Justin Kensington.

CHAPTER FOURTEEN

CORA HAD BEEN BATTLING the urge to call Ashley or Julia and tell them what she'd realized about Ethan. Part of her wanted to spill her guts and tell them she knew she was dating the wrong man, but every time she thought about telling them, she felt stupid. Stupid because she couldn't get over this foolish crush on a man who didn't want her and stupid because she was about to let a perfectly great guy slip away for some fantasy that could never happen.

So, she was doing the only logical thing. She planned to bury her feelings in a tub of the gooiest ice cream she could find. She'd wash that down with a family sized bag of something salty and oily, then top the whole thing off with chocolate milk. To her, chocolate milk was a comfort food. Ice cold and made with whole milk so it was thick and creamy and rich. Nothing was better.

Cora entered the convenience store at the gas station on the corner, fully prepared to binge shop so she could binge eat. The register was manned by a tall skinny kid Cora didn't know but recognized from having seen him working in the past. She smiled and headed toward the chip aisle, grabbing a bag of lime tortilla chips.

Dylan and Tommy ran up, greeting her with matching grins.

"Hi Miss Walker," Tommy said.

"What did one arm say to the other?" Dylan asked.

Cora laughed and met Alice's gaze behind the boys. Alice mouthed an apology. Cora gave a small shake of her head and followed the boys and their mother to the back where the frozen foods were kept.

"I don't know. What did one arm say to the other?" she asked, her mind still half on the topic of ice cream. She needed something with caramel.

"Let's play!" Dylan cracked up and Cora laughed. It was impossible not to. The boy thought he was hysterical.

She was focused on the ice cream selection when she realized there were muffled voices coming from the front of the store. Something about them didn't sound right. It took her mind what seemed like hours to process that something was wrong.

She looked toward Alice but time slowed to a standstill as her gaze caught on the glass of the refrigerated cases along the back wall.

In the reflection of the glass, she could see two men in ski masks. The shock of gunmetal flashed in their hands as Cora froze in place. This time, there wasn't any narrator in her head telling her where to find something to save herself and the kids. This was real life and she couldn't come up with some way to save them all.

Tommy and Dylan hadn't realized anything was wrong. They laughed and pointed to the popsicles in the case.

The kid working the register started crying and Cora saw the flash of confusion, then fear, on Tommy's face as he realized something was going on. Whether he'd heard the crying or just felt the electric tension in the air, she didn't know. Alice and Cora moved together, sweeping Dylan and Tommy into their arms.

All Cora could think was that she needed to cover the boys. She and Alice huddled in the back corner of the store, putting their bodies over the kids. Alice shushed the boys and told them to hold still.

There were shouts, the sound of heavy boots moving on the tile floor. Cora didn't look back. She bent over the boys, murmuring to them as she prayed any bullets wouldn't go through her and Alice into the boys. If she and Alice could just take all of them, the boys could walk out of there alive. She had no idea if that was possible. Maybe bullets would just go right through them.

Her stomach lurched and clenched, abject terror gripping at her. Cora braced herself for pain. The only thing she knew about guns was what she'd read in books or seen in movies. Would she hear the shot before the pain came? Or would her life end before she even felt it?

She closed her eyes, tears coming. She thought of her family, of never seeing them again. Of not getting to see her niece or nephew when it was born. God, how she wanted that.

A rough voice barked at the end of the aisle. "Keep your heads down and stay where you are."

Did that mean they wouldn't kill them? Would they let them live if no one looked at them?

The sound of the boys' sobs ripped at her.

Then there came the noise of the door opening and closing and the sound of the men running. She thought it was the men running, but she didn't dare move.

Alice was telling the boys not to move, and Cora could

hear the cashier crying. He was alive. She prayed he wasn't hurt.

She ducked her head, not daring to turn to look to see if the men were really gone. She heard sirens. Someone had either called the police or the cashier had hit an alarm or something.

She didn't move until the police entered and she heard her brother-in-law's voice. Seconds later, she felt his hands pulling her up. Garrett was there with two of his officers.

She felt her legs go weak and started to cry. She didn't stop for a very long time.

CHAPTER FIFTEEN

GARRETT HAD CALLED Cora's parents and her sister. One of them must have let her other sister and two brothers know. Ashley had been either smart enough or manipulative enough to bring Justin to the police station with her when she came.

Cora didn't care why he was there. She'd realized the minute she saw him that he was who she wanted to see. He was who she wanted with her right now.

Justin waited long enough to let her parents and siblings hug Cora, then he pulled her into his arms and held her tight for a long time. Nothing had ever felt so good.

"You sure you're okay?" he asked, echoing the question her family had asked ten times already.

"I am."

Justin crossed to where Alice sat with Dylan and Tommy. He kneeled and looked at the boys. "I heard you guys were really brave. Hey, Dylan, what do you call a cat in a haunted house?"

Dylan glanced at his mom, then shrugged his shoulders.

"A scaredy cat!" Justin said.

There was a pause and then Tommy started laughing, and Dylan followed close behind. Cora offered her hand in a high five to Justin. He slapped it, then repeated it when Tommy and Dylan offered their hands.

Alice pulled her boys to her side. "Garrett said we're free to go, so I'm going to get the boys home."

They said their goodbyes and walked out, and Cora hugged herself, thinking she should go now, too. She'd given her statement. She could get a ride home with her parents or one of her siblings.

Justin looked around and pulled her aside, away from her watching family. "Can we talk for a minute? In private?"

Cora looked over to her family. Her mother and Ashley were talking in the corner. Her brothers and father watched her and Justin like a pack of lions. Protective lions.

She shook her head at them and then walked to the other side of the room with Justin.

"I'm pretty sure this is as good as it's going to get for now."

Justin looked over her shoulder at her family, then looked at her. His face was unreadable. "I just want to tell you I'm glad you found someone who makes you happy. I've been an idiot. Not just with you dating lately, but with everything. I shouldn't have told you Ethan wasn't good enough for you. If he makes you happy, then he's good enough, no matter what I think."

Cora didn't know what to say. There was something sad in the way he was looking at her. She wanted to think it might be regret, but she wasn't about to head down the road of telling herself he might have feelings for her again. She'd told herself that too many times in the past and been disappointed.

Our heroine is developing a brain, dear readers.

He raised a hand to brush her cheek, the touch soft and gentle. "I should have..."

He didn't finish and she didn't want him to. Cora shook her head, not able to open her mouth to speak.

He should have done a lot of things.

"I'm glad you're safe," he finally said. "I'll see you Monday."

With one long look to her dad and brothers, he turned and walked out of the police station.

CHAPTER SIXTEEN

"OKAY, TALK TO ME." Ashley dropped onto the bed, crossing her legs in that criss-cross-applesauce kind of way preschoolers did. "I know what it's like to be that scared. I've been there, remember?"

Cora looked at Ashley. What Cora had been through was a drop in the bucket compared to Ashley's nightmare. Ashley had been kidnapped and had to fight her way out. She'd had to kill a woman to save herself and it was something that had taken Ashley a long time to come to terms with, but she was doing well now.

"I'm okay, really. I got lucky and they ran." The police had caught the men who'd robbed the convenience store. They'd been stupid enough to run a red light on the way out of the area. It caught the attention of an officer. When he radioed the plate in, it matched the plate reported by a witness who'd been outside the convenience store. They were in custody.

"Hey," Ashley put her hand on Cora's arm and waited for her sister to look up. "What you did took amazing guts. I'm so damned proud of you."

Cora was fighting tears for the tenth time that day. She'd been so damned scared and it seemed like her body was trying to cope with that with spontaneous bouts of crying. "Thanks, but there wasn't much of a choice. What was I going to do? There was no way I could run."

"You could have tried to hide yourself instead of covering those kids. You could have left Alice to deal with it on her own."

The sound that came from Cora was half grunt, half laugh. Running and hiding had never been an option.

"Now, you need to tell me what else is bothering you," Ashley said.

Oh hell, the tears came. Ashley was always able to read Cora's mind. It was a blessing and a curse to have a sister you were that close to.

Cora reached for a tissue and swiped at her tears, then blew her nose. She was an ugly crier. By now, her nose was probably bright red and she knew if she looked in the mirror she would see blotches on her cheeks.

"I think I'm more messed up than I thought."

Ashley reached out to touch Cora's hand. "What makes you say that?"

Cora blotted at her eyes again. "I always thought I had my past under control. I didn't do all of the stuff most people with abandonment issues do, you know? I wasn't jumping from relationship to relationship or glomming on to some guy and acting like we were ready to get married after two dates."

Ashley nodded. They'd all gone to therapy as kids. The term "abandonment issue" wasn't foreign to any of the Walker siblings.

"Then I realized I'd been holding out hope for *years* that Justin might wake up and see me someday, and Laura pointed out that that's probably as much of an abandonment issue as the other things."

"Yes, and you did something about that. You're seeing Ethan."

Cora pressed her eyes shut as more tears came. "I think I need to stop seeing Ethan."

"Why do you say that? I thought you liked him."

Cora sniffed and reached for another tissue. "I think I've known for a while now that he doesn't do it for me the way he should, but I didn't want to face it. I like him a lot, but it isn't more than friendship. When we kiss, I don't feel what I should. He can't sweep me away from reality or make my toes curl."

Ashley sighed. "The toe curl is kind of important."

Cora only cried harder at that and Ashley reached out to hold her. Sisters were the best.

She took a deep breath and said what she knew she needed to say. "I tried to like Ethan the way I should. I tried to make myself believe he could be the one, but he just isn't..."

She couldn't say it. She felt like a fool for even thinking it.

In a move of utter and complete lunacy, our heroine is still stuck on the one man she can't have.

"He isn't Justin." Ashley said it for her.

Cora nodded her head. "It's so stupid. I've never even kissed Justin, but I can't stop comparing every guy to him. When I met Lice Guy in the restaurant, the first thing I did was line him up to Justin in my head. I hate it."

Ashley scooted over next to Cora so they sat side-by-side. She wrapped an arm around her. "It's not stupid. I get it. But here's the thing. Just because Ethan wasn't the guy to make you forget Justin, doesn't mean there isn't a guy out there who will. One of these days, you'll meet someone whose kisses will make you forget all about Justin. You'll be like, Justin who?"

Cora nodded, looking down at her lap. "I just want that to happen now. I don't want to want him anymore."

"I know. But I promise, there's a guy out there for you. I'm an expert, remember?"

Cora laughed and leaned her head on Ashley's shoulder. They sat like that for a bit until her nose stopped running and the tears had dried up.

"What if this is just me switching to a new abandonment thing? Like, I stopped waiting for Justin, but now I'm going to head into no-guy-is-ever-good-enough territory and find reasons to reject every man who comes along?"

Ashley shook her head. "I don't think that's what you're doing. It's totally normal to date a few guys before you find the right guy for you. There's nothing unusual about that. It sucks, but it's life. Sometimes, even if your mom left you in a park and you spent a few too many years pining for one guy, you're still just a normal girl floundering in the dating pool like we all do."

Cora nodded and pressed the now-soggy tissue to her eyes again, taking a few deep breaths as Ashley rubbed her back.

"God, I hate to tell Ethan. He's got so much going on with his dad sick and the lawsuit and moving his business. It's shitty to be like, hey, it turns out you don't turn me on enough."

"Has he called? What happened at the convenience store must be all over town by now."

Cora pointed to her phone on the night stand. "He called and texted a couple of times. I told him I'm okay and I just wanted to sleep for a while."

"The fact he's okay with that tells me he knows on some level, at least, that you're not the one for him, either. When I told Justin what happened, I swear, he launched over his desk and flew through the door of his office to get to you. There was no doubt in my mind he was going to be coming to the police station with me. If you were the right woman for Ethan, he would be banging down your door right now to be sure you're okay."

Cora sat up and looked at Ashley. "You're confusing the hell out of me. I thought you said you thought I was going to meet someone someday who would make me forget Justin. Now you sound like you're saying Justin has stronger feelings for me than Ethan does."

Ashley's mouth twisted as she grimaced. "I think he does. I just think Justin's too fucked up in the head to realize what he feels. Or maybe it's just that he's too messed up to act on his feelings. Either way, I think you're right to move on. You can't wait for him forever."

Cora sighed. "God, I really hate that. I hate all of this."

Ashley pulled her to her and they sat, sisters, side-by-side. Neither had to say a word. It was enough just to be there together, knowing they had each other's backs.

CHAPTER SEVENTEEN

CORA SAT at the last light on the outskirts of town. She was going to tell Ethan that she didn't think they had a future together as anything other than friends. She'd do anything to avoid this kind of conversation, but she wasn't the type of person to play games or mess around. She wouldn't just make up excuses every time he asked her out until he got the point. She would suck it up and have the conversation.

Ethan had texted to see if she wanted to get lunch. She'd texted back that she wanted to talk to him. He had to know what was coming.

She pulled into the lot behind the feed store. He'd suggested they meet there and he was waiting, hands shoved in his pockets as he leaned against his car.

Cora parked and came out.

"Hey," she said.

"Hey," he said back.

Yeah, she hated this. She came to stand in front of him. "Ethan, I um..."

"Don't worry, Cora, I get it. You can skip the *it's not you, it's me* speech."

He didn't sound angry or bitter, just resigned. The knots in her stomach loosened a little as she realized he wasn't going to make a scene or try to convince her to give him more time.

"I'm really sorry, Ethan. If it helps, it really is all about me and not about you. I'm kind of hung up on someone." She thought about saying more, but if she said more, it would essentially be saying, *hey, you weren't enough to pull my attention away from him*. She clamped her mouth shut instead.

Ethan nodded. "Thanks."

"Still friends?"

His face relaxed and he smiled. "Yeah, I'd like that."

Cora hugged him and then walked to her car.

He called out to her when she'd reached the door. "Cora!"

She turned and looked at him. "Yeah?"

"I really do mean that, about being friends. I uh, I don't really have a lot of friends in the area anymore."

Cora grinned at him. "Well, you have one now."

CHAPTER EIGHTEEN

CORA TOOK a deep breath and knocked on Justin's door. She hadn't ever been to his house, but she knew where it was. Since it was a weekend, she'd taken a chance on finding him at home, although knowing him, he could just as likely be at work.

The door swung open to reveal Justin in a dark shirt and dark jeans, bare feet and mussed hair. She wondered if he'd been sleeping or maybe just tugging at his hair the way he sometimes did when he was stressed or thinking.

"Cora." The surprise was evident in his tone.

She raised a hand, palm out to stop him. "Are you alone?" She could picture herself having this soul baring monologue and then having some sexy slinky woman coming up behind him. Or his mother. Either would be mortifying and she wasn't about to do this with witnesses. It was bad enough the whole town knew she'd pined for him for years. The fact she was about to say what she was about to say would give them no end of gossip if it was overheard.

She didn't have to worry about any nosy neighbors over-hearing her. Justin lived in a large home set back on a secluded piece of land at the end of a half-mile long drive. It was the opposite of her duplex where she shared a porch with her neighbor on one side and could easily jump to her other neighbor's porch with a single leap.

He nodded, his expression half bewildered, half amused.

Another deep breath. "Okay, here's the deal. We all know I've been in lust with you for years. I mean, let's just be adults about this. I know it, the whole town knows it, and if you haven't figured it out by now, you're a complete idiot."

She narrowed her eyes and pointed a finger at him when he looked like he might interrupt her. "Let me get this out."

He waited.

"Everyone also knows I started dating other people. I was done waiting for you. I was finished with just living on a stupid pipe dream that wasn't going to happen."

Cora could see something brewing in his eyes, but she ignored the dark look. "So, I've gone on a few dates and suddenly you're taking an interest. So, I tell myself, don't be an idiot, Cora. Maybe he's suddenly thinking he wants what he can't have. That's no reason to go back to panting after him."

Justin opened his mouth. She put two fingers on his mouth. He stopped.

"So, I keep trying to make it work with someone else, even though, I'm no idiot. I try to make it work with these other guys. But the thing is, I'm also smart enough to see that something has been changing with you lately. I don't know what it is, but I can see the change. I can see that you're not pushing yourself to beat back some internal demon anymore. The demon that's always haunted you is gone. I can see that. And you tell me you're happy I found a man who makes me happy. You say it like you're sorry you missed your shot."

She stepped back now, letting her hand drop, to put some space between them. "But here's the thing. I don't know if that demon vanishing thing means you're ready to give something between us a try or whether you were never really interested in me in the first place and you only meant you were glad for me because we're friends."

Now she crossed her arms over her chest because she was suddenly realizing, as she spoke, that this could be a monumentally bad idea. She was probably going to walk away from this very embarrassed. What had started out as a well-rehearsed speech was devolving—very rapidly—into an epic babble fest.

"Anyway," she said, arms firmly clamped across her chest now like a barrier. "I just wanted to get that out there. Just in case there's any small chance you had changed your mind before I dive back into the dating pool."

She stopped and he looked at her for a minute. He didn't ask if she was finished. His expression said it all.

Cora waved her hand in a "go on," motion. Might as well get this over with.

Justin spoke slowly, but he took a step toward her as he did. His face was carefully blank.

"When you say, 'jump back into the dating pool,' does that mean you're out of it right now? As in, you're not seeing Ethan?"

Cora frowned. "No. Ethan and I are just friends now."

Justin moved before she finished the sentence. He closed the space between them and then, in a heartbeat, every damned fantasy she'd stored up over the years came true as his arms came around her. Cora's arms came up to his chest, her eyes wide as the mask over his face fell.

There, in his expression, she saw heat, vulnerability, and hope.

His motion slowed, and he simply stood there, holding her pressed to him as he lowered his head to hers, his mouth hovering inches from her own. When he spoke, his voice sounded gruff, almost strangled. "To answer a few of your questions, I've wanted you from the moment I saw you. Every time I saw you over the past three years, I've wanted to do this." He pulled her closer still. "To hold you like this."

"Oh." It was all Cora could think to say.

"And yes, things have changed recently. I honestly don't know how much of it had to do with seeing you date other men—which drove me out of my mind, by the way—and how much of it had to do with me finally talking to Laura and my mom about a lot of stuff that I should have faced years ago."

"Will you tell me about it?" Cora whispered. His mouth was so close to hers, she wanted to stand up on her tip-toes and close the distance, but she also wanted to protect her heart. She wanted to know he was really ready for this. That this was more than him just saying screw it, might as well since she's throwing herself at me.

That this was more than him just wanting to have her because he finally saw her walking away with another man.

Justin nodded, holding her for another minute, his mouth so close to hers, as he watched her closely. The heat in his eyes said he was thinking about kissing her, too.

He broke apart from her, slowly, not rushing as he took her hand and tugged her inside. He took her to the couch, where he sat, turned sideways to face her as he pulled her down next to him.

"What do you want to know?" he asked.

"All of it." She said the words, and despite their simplicity, she meant it. She wanted to know all of what he'd been figuring out lately. All of what he thought he wanted now. And all of what he thought he was ready for.

Justin blew out a breath as he ran a hand down his face. "I think I've been trying to make amends somehow for the last few years."

"For what?"

"For not saving my mom and Laura."

Cora shook her head. "You did save Laura. You were part of it, at least. You got shot trying to help her."

Years before, when Justin's sister-in-law had come to Evers, she'd been tracked by her former husband's partner. Justin had unwittingly helped him, not knowing the man wanted to hurt Laura. When that man went after Laura, Justin had stepped between her and a gun and taken a bullet in his gut because of it.

"Too little, too late. I grew up in a house where my father was emotionally controlling and physically abusing my mother. I didn't know. I knew they weren't happy in their marriage, and I knew I didn't want to have anything to do with my dad and his manipulating, controlling ways, but I didn't know about the abuse."

Cora stayed quiet now. She wanted to let him get this out, the same way he'd let her say her piece earlier. What he had to say was a lot harder and much heavier.

"By the time Laura joined our family, I had left home and was burying my head in the sand. My dad was dead, but somehow, his ghost still seemed to haunt the house for me. I was your typical spoiled rich kid. I blew enormous quantities of the family's fortune on fast cars and parties for people I barely knew. My mom never did anything to make me think she wanted me home and my brother and I weren't close. He was five years older than me and we'd gone to separate boarding schools as kids. My mom drank a lot. She was always taking pills to numb her own pain."

Justin's arm rested on his raised knee as he talked, his fingers playing with hers.

"I met Laura at the wedding, and then I took off again. I think I might have visited a total of two times while they were married and it never once occurred to me to wonder at the way she barely spoke. I never thought to ask why she seemed like a shell of a person being directed by my brother at every turn."

"I'm sure when you were there, your brother was on his best behavior."

Justin nodded. "He was. I still feel like I should have seen it. I should have known something was going on. Hell, I lived in my family's house with my mom and dad and never knew."

"No, you didn't. You said it yourself. You went to boarding school. How old were you when that started?"

Justin ran a hand down his face again. "Seven. First grade."

"See?"

"Yeah, I'm starting to get it. Laura and I have been talking a lot lately and my mom and I have talked about it. My mom says she was really good at hiding it from me. It's why she sent my brother and I away to school."

Cora took his hand. "You know what I think?"

One corner of his mouth twitched as he looked at her. "What's that?"

"I think you're holding yourself up to some imaginary standard that's completely unrealistic. You see, right now, you're a man who runs an organization focused on domestic violence. You're probably more knowledgeable about looking for signs of abuse than a hell of a lot of men out there. And you're looking back now on your childhood with the 20/20 vision of someone who can spot all the little tell-tale signs that a seven-year-old missed."

He watched her.

"But the thing is, you haven't made yourself see those events through the eyes of that seven-year-old kid."

He wove his fingers through hers and looked at her. "Don't take this the wrong way, but you sound a hell of a lot like my mom."

That brought a burst of laughter from Cora. "Gee, thanks."

He sobered and she realized he was watching her, but this time his gaze was on her lips, not her eyes. "I've wanted you from the moment I met you. I can see now that I was keeping my distance because I didn't think I deserved you. I didn't think I had the right to be happy and if there was one person who could make me happy, it was you. It *is* you."

Cora pressed her lips together. Her heart raced.

"I think some part of me worried, too, that I would turn out to be like my dad and my brother if I got married."

Cora scoffed. "That's just ridiculous."

He squeezed her hand where they were connected. "I'm going to start seeing a therapist about all this stuff. I think I've gotten it through my hard head that it's okay for me to be happy and that I'm not going to turn into a monster overnight just because my brother and father were monsters. I think, though, that it would be a good idea for me to see someone to make sure I don't start slipping and sabotage anything good that comes my way."

"Do you think something good is going to come your way?" Cora whispered.

Justin's eyes blazed with the heat and intensity she'd known he was holding at bay. He leaned in, closing the distance between them as her heart sped up and her toes started to feel the telltale signs that something toe-curling was about to happen.

He stopped, just long enough to whisper one more thing. "She already has."

And then he was kissing her and this kiss left no room for doubt or distraction or second-guessing. This kiss raced through her, sending her heart pounding, making certain parts of her warm, and curling her toes. Hell, she wasn't sure, but she thought she felt that curl all the way up to her calves.

CHAPTER NINETEEN

"WE'RE TAKING THINGS SLOW." Cora curled up on the couch, coffee in hand as Ashley took the other end and settled in.

"Just as long as that *slow* pace isn't going to match the three-year build up to your first kiss."

Cora couldn't help but laugh. "It better not." She looked down at her hands where they hugged the warm mug. "I do appreciate that he's taking the time to make sure he's got his head on right and everything. I think if we dove into this too quickly and then he realized he was only with me because it seemed like the right thing to do or something, it would kill me."

Ashley's grin was slow and filled with the mischief Cora was used to seeing there. "But he's an amazing kisser, right? I mean, did the toes curl?"

Cora laughed. "The toes totally curled." She tilted her head back. "Ah. May. Zing."

Ashley slapped a hand to her chest, in a dramatic gesture and sighed.

"Yeah, that's how I feel," Cora said, fanning herself.

"So, when are you going on an official date?"

"He's officially taking me out tonight, but he won't tell me what we're doing."

Ashley leaned in. "Oh, intrigue. I like it."

"I know, right? It's kind of fun not just doing a typical dinner date." She frowned. "At least, I assume it's not just going to be dinner."

It wasn't just dinner. Eight hours later, Justin rowed Cora out on Redding Lake in a row boat. A picnic basket sat between them and he was headed for the bend in the water where a small cove would give them even more privacy than the water already offered.

"You really put this picnic together yourself?"

Justin answered her with a grin.

She tried to lift the lid of the basket again. "And there's real food in there?"

"Hey! Hands off," he said, though his hands were stuck on the oars so he wasn't in a position to do anything to stop her.

Cora lifted her hands and laughed. "Just thought I'd check. You don't want to get me out on the water and have nothing to feed me. Appearances can be deceiving. I get hangry a lot more easily than you'd think."

He played at being offended. "It's not just peanut butter and jelly in there. I promise."

"Mm hmm."

He was telling the truth. When he unpacked it later, there *were* peanut butter and jelly sandwiches—which made her laugh—but there was also a bottle of wine, two glasses, fresh fruit salad, chips, pickles, and what looked like homemade apple pie.

Cora held up a sandwich. "I can't believe you cut the crusts off and cut them into triangles."

"Makes them taste better that way." Justin took hold of her wrist and brought her sandwich to his mouth, taking a large bite. "See? Perfect."

She shook her head. "White bread, too."

"Destroying peanut butter and jelly with whole grain stuff is sacrilege. There are some things in this world that we just don't do."

"I see." She took a bite of her sandwich and surveyed the food as she chewed and swallowed. "And are you going to sit here with a straight face and tell me you baked that pie?"

"Not at all." He was grinning now as he piled chips and a pickle next to the fruit on her plate. They were sitting knees to knees in the boat, plates balanced on their laps. "I bribed Laura. I promised her two hours of babysitting. I'll just call my mom when the time comes and ask her to come over so I don't screw anything up with Jamie."

Cora thought about saying that he wouldn't do anything to screw up Jamie. He was a great uncle, but she didn't say anything. She'd leave his therapist to do the work for him. She wasn't going to try to be his shrink and his girlfriend.

He loaded his plate, then looked at the wine and glasses, still sitting in the basket. "I'm not sure how we'll manage to balance our wine glasses if we set them down anywhere." He looked around. Between them and their plates and the basket, there wasn't a whole lot of space to put anything. "I also brought club soda, in case you didn't want wine. I wasn't sure what time of the month it was," he said with a wink.

Cora snorted. "I can make an exception and have a glass. We'll have to eat first, then drink wine," she said.

They did that, talking about nothing in particular as they ate. She enjoyed the peanut butter and jelly sandwiches more than she should have. She always made her own sandwiches on whole grain bread, and he was right. That was fine for turkey and cheese, but it sure didn't work for pb&j.

Justin packed their scraps and garbage back into the basket and handed her a glass of wine. "Scootch over," he said, standing and carefully balancing the boat as she slid to one side of her seat.

Cora gasped as the boat rocked and for a minute she thought they would both go over, but then he was settled on the seat next to her.

Wine had sloshed over the rim of her glass, landing on her hand. Cora licked the drops that ran onto her wrist, then heard a groan from Justin.

She looked over to find his eyes locked on her wrist.

"You need to stop that," he all but growled. It wasn't an angry growl. It was the kind of growl that said he was at the edge of his control.

She cleared her throat and lowered her hand. "Sorry."

"Ha!"

She grinned at that. He was right. She wasn't sorry. She appreciated that he wanted to do more with her than just make out, but she also liked the way she could make his eyes flash with lust. He'd been hiding that from her for so long, it was nice to finally see the effect she had on him.

He slid an arm around her and buried his head in her neck, groaning again. "SO damned tempting. You smell like jasmine."

She flushed. "It's my soap. I love jasmine. I'm surprised you can identify the smell. I would bet most men can't."

"I have a lot of hidden skills."

"Like ninja skills?" she asked.

"Yep. My hidden ninja jasmine identifying skills." He sipped his wine. "I'm thinking of making a bucket list."

"Yeah?" She looked over at him. The sun was sinking in the sky and this side of the lake was quiet and peaceful. The sounds of laughter and kids playing came from the other side where a family campground and a long row of hunting cabins lined half of it. Getting over to the side they were on meant crossing through a lot of private land. Justin had gotten permission from the owners to cross through their gates and use their access ramp to the water.

"I'm going to start working less and bring more people in to the charity to take some of the load off of my desk."

His shoulders, was more like it. He'd taken too much on for far too long and she knew he took it as a personal obligation more than a job.

"I would have thought you'd crossed a lot of things off your bucket list when you were younger. Didn't you say you were hopping from country to country partying?"

Justin grimaced. "Yeah, it was pretty gross. But I think I can fill this bucket list with more meaningful things than blowing through money I did nothing to earn as fast as humanly possible."

"Like what?"

He looked at his wine glass in the dimming light. "I'm not sure."

Cora couldn't help but laugh, and when he scowled, she laughed harder.

Eventually, she reached across the boat, feeling Justin put a steadying hand on her lower back as she did, and grabbed her purse. She handed her wine glass to him and dug in her bag for the small pad of paper and pen she kept there.

She tossed her purse back to its spot and took her glass from Justin, settling the pad in her lap.

"Let's see," she said, thinking for a minute. She wrote on the pad, covering it with her hand.

"Are you writing my bucket list for me?"

"I am."

He waited while she scribbled some more things and then took the notepad with a skeptical look and read aloud. "Spend the night in a haunted place."

He looked at her. "I like that one."

She offered a smug smile and he went back to the list.

"Drive across the United States. Learn to bake an apple pie." He looked at her again. "Wiseass."

She bumped him with her shoulder. "Keep reading."

"Sleep under the stars. Get a dog."

He'd reached the end of the list.

"It's a work-in-progress," she said. "We'll add to it as we go."

He took the pencil from her hand and wrote on the page before taking her wine glass. He set the empty wine glasses in the basket and showed her the list.

"Kiss Cora Walker in a boat," Cora read, then flushed, her cheeks heating.

Justin tossed the pencil and the notepad into the basket and put one hand on her cheek, drawing her to him with the lightest of touches.

She leaned into him as her lips parted and she was pretty damned sure she sighed. He brushed his lips against hers, so softly that she wasn't sure he was touching her, but damned if it didn't do things to her anyway.

"I like my list," he said, then closed in and kissed her deeply. A long, slow kiss that told her just how much he liked the last addition to the list.

Cora moaned and tried to get closer to him. He lifted one of her legs and laid it across his lap, and she slid fully onto his lap. The sky had been growing darker and now the sun fell beneath the horizon as his hands moved over her and their bodies rocked together on the water.

CHAPTER TWENTY

"DO YOU NEED HELP?" Ashley asked as Cora stood to head to the kitchen.

Cora smiled at her sister. Ashley and Garrett sat on the couch. Justin was in the armchair. They were having dinner together.

Our heroine is buzzing with excitement. Cora's internal narrator wouldn't shut up, despite the fact she'd shown she had no talent for writing like Ashley.

Still, Justin had given her some ideas for some of the more exciting scenes in Ashley's books. Not the shoot-em-up kind of excitement. The between-the-sheets kind of excitement.

"No, I got it. About ten more minutes for the rice to finish and we can eat." She was making tofu with an Indian curry sauce.

The smells filling the house told her it was going to be good. She planned to add extra spice to Justin's serving since he liked spicy food.

She checked the rice, then stirred the curry simmering in a pan. She pulled a large portion out and put it in a separate pan and began adding the seeds from the chilis she'd used in the initial sauce. She would let those cook down and then add a little chili oil, as well. It was some kind of chili oil she hadn't heard of before but she'd found it in the hot sauce section of the grocery store and hoped it would be good.

"Garrett, do you like your curry spicy?" She called out. She already knew Ashley didn't.

"Sure, spice is good!" Garrett called back.

She didn't want to change the underlying flavors of the sauce too much, but she wasn't used to cooking spicy foods, so she wasn't sure how much to add. She added what she thought of as a small dash of chili oil and then turned the temperature down and left it simmering on the stove before going back into the living room.

"I haven't felt sick for the last couple of weeks, so I'm hoping it's over," Ashley was saying. She and Garrett were beyond excited about the baby. Come to think of it, the whole family was.

Ashley had been pregnant once as a teenager but she'd lost the baby during a violent attack from her foster father. This pregnancy would be different. This one was filled with hope and love and nothing but excitement for the baby to come.

"I can't wait to shop for tiny baby clothes," Cora said, smiling at Ashley. "You know you have to find out what the baby is, so we can start shopping soon."

"It's gonna be human, I'm pretty sure. At least, I think so," Ashley said.

"Wiseass." Cora didn't tell Ashley she'd already bought an adorable pair of ivory baby shoes that could be worn by either a boy or a girl. She couldn't resist. They were too cute for words.

Ashley grinned at her. "They'll do another ultrasound in two weeks. As long as the baby is turned the right way and everything, they should be able to tell at that visit."

Cora's phone beeped marking the end of the timer she'd set for the rice. She stood. "That's the rice."

The others all stood and everyone followed her into the kitchen. She didn't have a large dining room table to entertain guests at, so they'd be eating at her kitchen table.

She piled rice onto the plates and then spooned tofu and vegetables onto the plates, giving Garrett and Justin the spicier version of the curry. She set dishes of each of the curries on the table so people could get seconds if they wanted them. She also had a basket of naan bread she'd bought at the store and warmed up set in the middle of the table.

Conversation was light and easy as they sat down to eat, but Cora was nervous, just the same. She wondered if it had been stupid to suggest the double date. Maybe it was too soon to be doing such *couple-ish* things. Was she pushing this along too hard, too fast? Would Justin run if he felt too much pressure?

Garrett coughed and took a sip of his beer and Cora realized Justin was doing the same.

"Oh no, did I make it too spicy?"

Justin waved away the question. "No, it's good." He went back to eating, but she thought it might be with just a little too much gusto.

Garrett took a spoonful of the milder version of the curry and mixed that with the curry on his plate. Before he continued eating.

The conversation had stopped as Cora and Ashley watched the men eat. Cora knew she'd added too much chili oil. That was becoming abundantly clear as Justin continued to clear his throat a lot and a small sheen of sweat broke out on his forehead.

"Justin, you don't have to eat it. There's plenty of the mild one left if you'd rather have that." Cora fidgeted in her seat.

Ashley laughed. "Aww, he's making himself eat your crappy cooking."

"I'm not a crappy cook!" Cora said.

"I love it," Justin offered. Cora and Ashley ignored him. Garrett was damned near having an aneurism laughing at Justin at this point.

Justin drank more beer.

"You're not normally a crappy cook," Ashley continued, as though the dinner wasn't devolving into some bizarro *see-how-red-Justin-can-get* show. "But, apparently, you don't know how to make something spicy without killing people."

"Your nose is running," Garrett said to Justin. Garrett had given up and added even more of the mild curry to his plate, stirring it into the concoction.

Justin just shook his head and kept going.

"It is sweet that he's eating," Ashley murmured.

Cora tried to pull the plate away but Justin held it in place. "It's good, Cora, really."

His voice came out a bit more croaky than it should have been. He sounded more like an amphibian than a man at this point.

Cora chewed her lip and watched Justin as he grabbed for the naan and tried to use that to counter the spice.

Ashley and Garrett were both laughing now.

Justin took one more bite and seemed to put a great amount of effort into chewing and swallowing it, but she could see the sweat growing on his face.

He held out about three more seconds before breaking

for the refrigerator and grabbing the milk carton. He chugged straight from the carton.

Maybe he'd gotten a mouthful with one of the dashes of straight chili oil she'd sprinkled on his plate just before serving it.

CHAPTER TWENTY-ONE

IT WAS all over the town by noon. A group of kids playing at one of the houses near Mr. Knight's property had found a metal drum sticking up out of the ground. Actually, it was only the corner of a drum. The rest of it had been buried deep under the ground.

When the mom came out to see what the kids were banging on, she'd realized it might be related to the well poisoning and she'd called the police. They'd called in a state agency to look into it, and ten rusted barrels had been recovered from the site.

"I doubt we'll know anytime soon whether they're related to the furniture company, but they have to be, don't you think?"

Cora listened as the women behind her in the diner talked. She was waiting for Laura, Ashley, Julie, and Presley to join her for lunch.

"There's no way it's not related. I mean, really," another woman said, "the furniture company had that storage facility out that way and now, these show up buried not ten miles down the road?"

The two women were standing now, gathering their things. Cora looked up as her friends came from the other direction and sat down, Ashley taking the seat beside Cora, and Laura, Julia, and Presley slipping in across from her.

It didn't take long for the conversation to move to the drum discovery at their own table.

"Okay, who has details to share?" Ashley asked.

"I thought you would know," Presley said. "You're married to the Chief of Police."

Ashley shook her head. "He's too by-the-book for me to get anything out of him."

"I heard the containers were too rusted to have any labels or anything like that, but there are some numbers stamped right into the metal," Julia said. "I bet those match the furniture company."

Presley closed her menu and put it down. Cora wondered why she even looked at it. They'd all eaten at the diner so many times, there was no way they didn't have the menu memorized.

"They do." Presley looked around like it was normal for her to have detailed information. It wasn't at all normal.

Presley and her boyfriend, James, both tended to steer clear of gossip. They were by far the most reserved people in their group of friends, choosing to stay home often, even when the whole group went out. James suffered from some serious PTSD so social situations could be hard on him.

"I went over to the site this morning," Presley said. "I wanted to see how far it was from the ranch so we'd know if we need to worry about this affecting the horses."

"Oh, that's good thinking," Ashley said.

Presley was a former grand prix horse jumper. She kept her horse over at Bishop Ranch, the ranch owned by Laura's husband's family. It made sense that she'd have wanted to know right away if the discovery of buried chemicals might threaten her horse's safety.

"They weren't letting people near the site, of course, but you could see what they were doing from the road." She shrugged a shoulder. "It was interesting."

"So, how did you find anything out?" Cora asked. She'd thought of calling Ethan. He lived two houses over from where the drums had been found, and they were probably on land that once belonged to his family. She just hadn't felt right calling for details when his dad was likely sick because of those drums.

"I overheard some of the workers talking as they were leaving. They didn't seem to notice that I was listening. One guy said the furniture company was screwed now and the other guy said a company representative was already scrambling to show those drums were turned over to a legitimate transport company who was supposed to take them to a disposal facility."

Cora frowned. "I wonder if they can prove that."

"I hope so," Ashley said. "I know what's happened to Mr. Knight is horrible, but I hate to think what will happen to all the people who work for the company if they shut down."

"It's not just Mr. Knight anymore," Cora said. "There are two kids on neighboring properties that were checked into the hospital. I haven't heard what their exact diagnoses are, but I don't think it's good."

They were interrupted by Gina. "Hey ladies, we're out of potatoes and I don't have any more meatloaf, but the chicken sandwich today is to-die-for. Tina made a new secret sauce for it, and it's going to make the menu permanently, it's so good."

The women looked at each other for a stunned second.

Even though the food the sisters served was all fantastic, they rarely added anything new to the menu.

"The chicken sandwich, please," they said in unison.

"Four chicken sandwiches," Gina said. "Ice teas all around?"

The women nodded.

Three days later, Cora pulled up in front of Mr. Knight's house and got out of her car. The people from the state had left, but they'd sealed off a large area of what used to be Mr. Knight's land and there were warning signs to keep people out. Cora would bet plenty of people had ignored the signs and any risk the barrels of crud might pose and went snooping anyway.

She thought about skipping her Sunday delivery of muffins to Mr. Knight. Now that she knew Ethan was here living with him, she didn't really need to come out and check on him or keep him company. Plus, it was a little weird since she'd had a few dates that went nowhere with Ethan. Still, they said they'd be friends and his dad had come to expect Sunday muffins. She hated to let him down.

She took the plastic container out of the passenger seat, but left her purse and phone sitting on the seat. In the hill country, you didn't need to worry about whether someone would steal your purse or your car when you went to visit someone. Not this far from town, at least.

She'd doubled the muffin recipe this time, knowing Ethan and his dad would be fighting over them. Ethan's truck wasn't in front of the house, so she guessed he was working in town or out running errands.

She knocked on the door, but it swung open when she did. "Mr. Knight?" She called out and stepped into the house. She'd found the door open plenty of times before and didn't think anything of it. She should mention to

Ethan that the door latch didn't catch well. He could probably fix it for his dad.

"Mr. Knight, it's Cora Walker!"

She walked through the entryway and turned toward the den to see if he was in his chair napping. He liked to sit in the beat-up armchair in front of the television, even though he rarely watched any shows.

A shadow at the bottom of the stairs caught her eye as she turned and she changed course, heading deeper into the hallway toward the staircase.

"Mr. Knight?"

A crumpled form lay at the bottom of the stairs, still and silent. Dread and shock warred in Cora's gut as she realized it was Mr. Knight.

"Mr. Knight!"

Cora dropped the muffins and her bag in the hall as she ran to his side.

Full understanding dawned as she saw the blood. He was facing away from her, but when she came close, she saw the gash in his forehead. It was swollen and bruised and blood pooled beneath him.

There was no doubt in her mind he was dead. She couldn't say whether it was in the stillness of his body or the ashen pallor of his face. She reached out and felt at his neck anyway, but the movement took force. She didn't want to do it.

He wasn't cold, per se, but she could tell his body wasn't as warm as it should be either. Some part of her wanted to go get a blanket to cover him up, but she stopped herself. There was no pulse. He wasn't breathing.

Cora was shaking as she left the house to get her phone in the car. Her hands were no steadier when she dialed her brother-in-law's phone number and told him what she'd found. Since Garrett was the Chief of Police, she hadn't bothered with nine-one-one.

"I don't suppose I need to tell you not to touch anything?" Garrett asked. "It doesn't sound like anything other than an accident, but..."

He didn't need to finish the sentence. Her brother-in-law had been a major crimes detective in a nearby city before coming to Evers. He would follow protocol with any dead body.

A shiver ran through her at the thought of the body inside the house. Poor Mr. Knight had been so sick lately, but that didn't make his death any easier to face.

"Garrett, his son is probably working at the feed store today."

"I'll go there first. I'm sending an ambulance and Carter out your way, though. I'll call Ashley and have her come, too."

"Thanks, Garrett." He was right. She wanted her sister.

Truthfully, Justin flashed through her mind first and she wanted to call him, but she couldn't bring her current boyfriend out here when Ethan would be coming home.

Ethan was about to find out his father was dead. She should be here for him. She could go see Justin as soon as she'd been a friend for Ethan.

CHAPTER TWENTY-TWO

CORA SAT with Ethan on the porch steps after the ambulance and police cars had pulled away. Garrett hadn't found anything to indicate that Ethan's father hadn't died as a result of an accidental fall from the top of the stairs. Mr. Knight had been getting weaker and weaker, so he'd likely either suffered a dizzy spell and lost his balance, or simply slipped trying to come down the stairs.

Ashley had offered to stay with Cora and Ethan but Cora sent her home. There was nothing she could really do to help. Pretty soon, the neighborhood patrol would come around with casseroles. The town of Evers might have been upset at Mr. Knight's lawsuit against one of its major employers, but they would be there for his son while he mourned. It's what small towns did.

"I tried to get him to let me move a bed to the den for him, but he wouldn't do it." Ethan sounded hollowed out, like he was still trying to figure out what had happened. He was white as a sheet and his hands shook just a little. You had to look closely to see it, but it was there.

Cora had a feeling the fact his father was gone hadn't truly sunk in yet. This had been expected. The doctors had said that with the damage to his body from the chemicals he'd been exposed to, he wouldn't last long. Still, she could guess Ethan thought he'd have time to say goodbye. No one had expected it to end so suddenly.

She rubbed Ethan's back. "I'm so sorry, Ethan."

He brushed at a tear that ran down his face and nodded.

Cora murmured something she hoped was comforting, but she didn't know what to say to make this better for him. She thought about saying his father wasn't in pain anymore and that was a good thing, but she didn't think anyone ever really wanted to hear those words when they'd lost a loved one.

"I can't believe this happened." He'd said the same thing a few times now, and she still had no response for him. "I think I didn't really think he would..." He didn't finish the sentence.

"Do you want me to get you something to eat or drink?" She looked over at the old porch swing. She wasn't sure it was safe to sit in, but Ethan probably wouldn't want to go into the house yet. His father's body was gone, and Ashley had cleaned the blood at the bottom of the staircase before she and Garrett left, but how could he look at that hallway again and not see his father's body lying there?

"You can sit out here," she said, motioning to the swing, "and I'll bring something out to you."

Ethan looked at her, then, this time not trying to wipe the tears from his face. "Will you just sit with me for a while?"

Cora nodded. Her heart broke for him. His mother had died when he was little. Now his father was gone. She didn't know if he had any other family, but even if he had aunts or uncles or grandparents that were still alive, he'd just lost the last of his immediate family. Cora knew what it was like to be alone in the world.

She could sit with him. If there was anything she could do right then to make him feel better, she would.

CHAPTER TWENTY-THREE

"THANK YOU." Cora took the last of the dishes Justin handed her and lowered them into the sudsy water in the sink. She loved the feel of the warm bubbles. She was probably a little strange, but she liked washing dishes. She'd never fought with her siblings over that chore.

Others, yes. When it was time to rake the lawn or fold the laundry, she'd be the first to claim it wasn't her turn, but washing dishes was something she was willing to do anytime.

Justin had tried to tell her he'd do them since she had cooked, but she wanted the calm right now.

"When is the funeral?" he asked, taking the clean dishes she'd set in the drain board and drying them. Cora's small duplex didn't have a dishwasher. She thought he might comment on it, but he didn't seem to mind.

"I'm not sure yet," she said. "Probably in a few days."

"Let me know when it is, and I'll go with you."

Cora looked at him. "You wouldn't mind?"

"No. I understand you want to be there for Ethan. I want to be there for you."

Cora nodded, pulling the drain plug in the sink and watching the water wash down the drain.

Justin reached to put a frying pan on the shelf above the toaster oven. He'd watched her cook the meal, so he must have noted where she was pulling things from.

"A lawyer for Caufield's Furniture held a press conference," he said. "They said they will be able to produce a paper trail showing the metal drums that were dug up had been turned over to a transportation company that was hired to transport them to a chemical disposal company. He said the company demonstrated no negligence in the handling of their chemical waste. Even if they do show that, the cost of defending the suit long enough to clear them might take down a company of their size. They seem like a large company to the town, but on a national scale, they aren't huge."

Cora wiped her hands on a dish towel and they moved together to the living room to sit side-by-side on the couch.

She was glad for the strong arms and heat that wrapped around her as he pulled her toward him.

"I'm sorry you had to go through that today."

She was sitting with her back to his chest. When he spoke, he lowered his head to graze a kiss across her neck.

She didn't answer him. She moaned softly and tilted her neck to grant him greater access. This was what she needed. This was what would make the image of Mr. Knight's broken body lying at the bottom of the stairs go away.

"Cora." It was a whisper as he moved his hands to run up and down her arms. His mouth traveled up her neck to her jaw and then she turned in his arms and his mouth covered hers.

Cora lost herself in his kiss. His body was hard and unyielding beneath her and she could feel the evidence of what this kiss was doing to him. She was glad. She hated to think its effect was one-sided. It was a hell of an effect. Cora had gone soft and warm at his touch. Every part of her felt like a lightning strike of pleasure had run through her, sparking desire and need.

She ran her hands over his chest as his hands found their way to the buttons on her shirt. He was undoing them, but his pace was maddening. Cora wanted to take over for him, if only she could pull her hands away from him long enough to be effective.

She didn't want to stop running her hands over him, though. The only thing better than touching his chest would be touching his bare chest.

She slid her hand under his shirt, feeling hot flesh over tight muscle. She meant to go to his chest, but her hand stalled on a six pack of abs that made her groan.

She could feel his lips pull into a smile as he broke their kiss but kept their mouths connected. "Right back at you, baby."

Cora laughed but the sound was cut off when he put an arm around her and flipped them, rising over her on the couch. He leaned on an elbow and reached with his other arm to grab the couch pillows and toss them over the back side of the couch, giving them more room.

She lifted the hem of his shirt and he took over, pulling it over his head and off. Cora felt like she might swallow her tongue. The man was incredible. She wouldn't have guessed he would be this cut under those buttoned-up shirts he wore to the office all day. She made a mental note to ask him what he had to do to maintain this body, then promptly lost herself in the feeling of his body moving over hers.

He kissed her as their hips ground together. Cora broke from his mouth and kissed the warm skin of his shoulder, then ran her mouth down his chest, letting her tongue explore as he hissed in a breath.

He caught her hand and held it in place. "We need to slow down or I won't be able to stop."

Cora grinned. There was something incredibly powerful in knowing she was pushing him to the point of losing control. There was also something incredibly moving in knowing he wanted to hold back with her. They'd talked about not wanting to jump right into bed even though they'd known each other for years.

She liked that, but it was a little hard to stick with that decision at a time like this.

He rolled to his side and pulled her to him, then lazily kissed her as his hands trailed over the skin he'd exposed above her bra.

"I like this," he said. "I like just holding you and touching you and knowing it doesn't need to go any further than this right now."

"Me, too," she said, and she meant it. It might seem a bit like high school to make out for hours, without even taking off all of their clothes, but she didn't care. It felt right for them right now, and that's what she cared about. This felt very right.

CHAPTER TWENTY-FOUR

"HOW DO YOU KNOW ALL THIS?" Cora looked at Justin as he explained another self-defense move.

"You're a horrible student." He stood in front of her in his office wearing pressed slacks and a white button-down shirt rolled up at the sleeves. He'd kicked off his shoes.

"True, but I'm not convinced this can be considered work." So far, they'd spent the last hour with him showing her several self-defense moves and then making her practice them. "I'm supposed to be working for you."

Justin scowled. "Yeah, well this is what I want you focusing on today."

Cora crossed her arms and gave him one of her best teacher stares. He didn't fall for it.

"What if one of those guys at the convenience store had decided they needed a hostage to help them get away?"

Cora felt cold wash down her spine at the idea but she stood up straighter and looked him in the eye. "I would have gone with them, Justin. I know that's not what you want to hear, but I would have done it because it would have drawn them away from the kids." She stepped to him and reached out to touch his arm. "I'm sorry, but I can't tell you I wouldn't have done that."

Justin sighed and pulled her into a hug. "I figured that." He let go and went to his desk. "That's why I got you this."

He opened a drawer and pulled out a canister of pepper spray or mace on a keychain and another keychain with a small pendant on it. He held them both up to her.

"Pepper spray that dyes your attacker's face blue to mark them." He held up the pendant. "A personal alarm. Put this one on the outside of your purse so you can easily grab it and pull it loose if you're attacked."

Cora took both items and studied them, then set them back on the desk before going to him. She put both hands on Justin's face and looked him in the eye. "Thank you. I will absolutely use them, and I'll even keep practicing self-defense techniques with you, but I need you to know that nothing's going to happen to me. It was scary and horrible, but I'm okay now."

He covered her hands with his own and nodded.

"Now," she said, with a grin, "tell me where you learned all these moves."

He laughed. "You remember when I was blowing through my family's fortune?"

She smirked. "From what I understand, you might have spent hundreds of thousands of dollars on your own, but you barely put a dent in it."

He shrugged. "True. Anyway, shortly before my brother was killed, I started to get tired of being drunk all the time. I had a friend who knew Muay Thai and some Aikido. I asked him to teach me some things. I was thinking that I would go to Thailand and study the method. I think I envisioned myself moving from one country to the next in some quest for..." he shook his head, "I don't know, something. I would study one martial art after the other until I found myself. It was stupid. Anyway, I learned enough from him to be slightly useful in a fight before I got the call that my brother had died."

"You always make it sound like it was your brother's death that made you turn your life around."

Now it was his turn to smirk. "I was hardly doing anything noble. I was prepared to spend another small fortune traveling the globe a second time, only this time I planned to study martial arts instead of cocktail mixology. Hardly noble."

Her eyes burned fierce. "It was something. You like to pretend you were this worthless person, but when you saw the evidence of Laura's abuse, what did you do?"

"I went after her. I wanted her to know we would be on her side from that point on. I didn't want her to think she needed to raise her baby alone. Or that she needed to fear us."

Cora laced her arms behind Justin's neck and stood on tip toe to kiss him. "Whether you like it or not, Justin Kensington, you're a good man. And I have a sneaking suspicion you always have been."

CHAPTER TWENTY-FIVE

JULIA AND CORA left the small apartment they'd rented on an online site. It was a tiny one room studio over a garage in an Austin neighborhood known as Hyde Park. The price had been right for two teachers on a budget, and they hadn't minded sharing the single queen bed for two nights while they shopped.

It wasn't July fourth weekend. They'd decided to move their shopping trip up a bit and Cora was glad they had. She'd gotten her hair cut the day before, opting for a cut that brought the length up to her shoulders and added layers framing her face. She loved it.

"Oh, I almost forgot," she said, digging into her purse after they'd settled into Julia's car. "Justin got us a gift card for a restaurant so we can splurge on dinner tonight." She pulled out the printed gift card he'd sent to her email as a surprise.

Julia looked over and made an appreciative oohing sound. "I love that man."

"Hands off," Cora said with a mock scowl, drawing a laugh from her friend.

"Okay," Julia said. "I want to check out that boutique Ashley told us about and then maybe we can go get makeup?"

Cora nodded and bit her lip. "Um, can we uh also..."

Julia laughed. "Did you have something to say, Cora?"

Cora flushed. She didn't want to say it.

Julia put on a prim affect. "Why yes, Cora. We *can* go to a dirty lingerie store so you can get some naughty panties for your boyfriend."

Her cheeks heated further and she mumbled a response that might have included threats against Julia's favorite pair of shoes.

Julia only laughed harder, but she did help Cora choose three nighties with lace and frilly see through spots and all kinds of things that Cora couldn't wait to wear for Justin someday. She also picked three new sets of lace bras and panties. One was a demi bra that cut low and showed off her breasts in a way she hoped would make Justin lose control.

They'd been seeing each other for a month now and she thought she was ready to move past the "taking things slow" stage.

She had a feeling he was, too. Things had been heating up lately and walking away at the end of a night of making out seemed to be as hard for him as it was for her.

"Makeup?" Julia asked, as they left the lingerie section after ringing up their purchases. Cora nodded. She'd spent her savings on a few cute skirts and dresses at the boutique and put the lingerie purchases on her credit card. She'd budgeted for fifty dollars in new makeup. She couldn't get much with that nowadays, but she wanted to get a new blush and some new eye shadows.

"So, I take it you've taken yourself off all the online

dating sites?" Julia asked as they took the escalator down to the cosmetics department.

"Of course." Cora looked over at her friend. "Why wouldn't I?"

Julia shrugged. "I just know you didn't do that when you were dating Ethan. It's different with Justin?"

Cora pressed her lips together and nodded. "It really is." She looked down as they stepped off the escalator and then glanced away from her friend. "It is for me, at least."

Julia put a hand on Cora's arm, pulling her to the side. "Hey, what's that face for? Do you think it's not as big of a deal for him?"

"I don't know. I mean, I think it is, but I guess I worry sometimes that maybe it's not? I mean, what if he decides this isn't doing it for him or he changes his mind or..."

Julia struck that Mama Bear pose she sometimes took with the kids. "Hey, listen to me, Cora."

Cora's eyes met Julia's.

"Listen good, okay? I get that sometimes you have left-over—" Julia waved her hands around— "shit from your mom walking away from you like that. I know it affects you sometimes, and all, but I also know you're smart. So, I need you to use your head to check yourself when things start to creep in and worry you."

Cora didn't answer, but her focus was fully on Julia now.

"You guys have been together about a month now, right?"

One month and six days. Cora had been counting. She nodded.

"You've been making out but haven't had sex."

Cora raised her brows. "You know the answer to that."

They'd talked about it.

Julia made an exasperated face. "Listen, chickie, if he was planning to leave, he'd either leave or he'd screw you and then leave."

Cora took a slow breath. She knew Julia was right. Still, it didn't mean he wouldn't leave someday. That this wouldn't someday end.

Julia started the mind reading thing again. "And yes, he might leave someday. Maybe you guys will find out that this isn't the right thing for you down the road, but you can't live life that way. You can't live life wondering if things are going to end. If you do that, you miss the good stuff. You miss the *now*."

Julia leveled Cora with a look. "You know I'm right, right?"

Cora laughed. "You're right."

And she was. They moved on to makeup, and Cora focused on letting herself enjoy the *now*. Julia was right. She wouldn't let her mother's actions govern her life. She wouldn't let her mom and her failures take over. She'd gone after what she wanted with Justin. She wanted it to work out, and she'd do all she could to make sure it did work out. She would work for her future with him, but she wouldn't let herself fall into the trap of worrying about *what ifs* anymore. She would enjoy the *now*.

CHAPTER TWENTY-SIX

JUSTIN OPENED the door for Cora, letting her slip past him into the house.

"That restaurant was worth the drive." She kicked her heels off her feet and left them laying by the door.

She felt his arms come around her after he shut the door. Cora sank back into him, tilting her head as his mouth traveled over the skin of her neck. She moaned and lifted her arms to run her hands through his hair.

It was surreal, being here with him. She couldn't believe it was really happening. She'd made an appointment that morning with the therapist she'd seen years before. She'd realized lately that maybe she did have a few leftover issues from her childhood. She'd be damned if she was going to let any of her hang-ups get in the way of this working out.

He ran his hands down her arms and his fingers caught her hand and pulled her behind him to the couch. When he sat, he settled her across his lap, bringing his mouth to hers again.

His eyes seemed darker somehow, as he broke the kiss

and looked at her. When he spoke, his voice had the low timbre of heat and need.

"I'm so damned glad I stopped being a dumbass."

Cora couldn't help it. She tipped her head back and laughed. "I'm pretty happy about that, too."

Then he was kissing her again and her thoughts turned to mush as pure feeling and sensation took over. Every part of her seemed to tingle and vibrate with pleasure.

When his hands slid down her back, her hands slid up his torso to his chest. It wasn't enough. She wanted more.

She tugged at his shirt, on fire with the need to feel him without clothes or barriers between them.

When he pulled his shirt over his head, Cora sat back and absorbed the sight of him. He was incredible. Tanned skin with a smattering of blond hair on his chest. Muscles tight with what she hoped was sexual tension and not stress of some other kind.

She ran a finger down his chest to his abs, letting it trail over all the dips and valleys of the cut muscles.

He hissed a response when she dawdled at the hem of his pants. "You're killing me, Cora."

She looked up, meeting his eyes. "I want you."

With a groan, he wrapped her tight in his arms, pulling her body to meet his, capturing her mouth again.

"Please," she whispered. No, whimpered. She was a pleading mess now.

"Are you sure?"

"Yes. Absolutely."

Justin stood, lifting her with him and walking back toward the bedrooms. She'd never seen more than the living room and kitchen of his house, but when he entered a bedroom, she knew at once that it was his.

Dark burgundy and navy bed linens stood out against

pale gray walls. There were black and white photos on the walls. Later, she would look at them and see that they were taken in all the places he'd traveled around the world. Some showed famous monuments, but most showed things you wouldn't find in a commercial print. The doorway of a church or the slanted crumpling roof of an old cottage.

Anticipation swirled deep in her belly. There was, without a doubt, toe curling happening.

Justin laid her on the bed, coming down over her. His hands and mouth worked in tandem as he stripped her bare. She wriggled, wanting to cover herself from him, but when she looked in his eyes, she saw nothing but a very distinctive male pride.

He stood, holding her gaze as he unbuttoned his pants, and she realized, she was all but drooling. Her mouth watered at the sight of him shucking his pants and boxers.

Warm flesh met hers when he crawled over her. "I want you to know, Cora, there was never a time when I didn't want this, want you. From the minute I saw you, I wanted you."

She was helpless to answer. She couldn't have formed words in that moment for anything.

His mouth moved from one breast to the other, kissing and licking between his words.

"But, this, Cora. I never could have imagined this."

She ran her nails lightly up his back, lifting her hips to urge him closer to her.

He broke away from her and she felt his absence keenly. But then he shifted to the nightstand and opened a drawer, and she processed what he was doing. A condom.

It was a good thing one of them was thinking right now.

He lay on his back to roll the condom on, and she

couldn't resist. She nipped his shoulder with her teeth, then soothed the spot with her tongue.

He growled and shot her a warning look, but she just laughed. She felt completely free with him. She thought she'd be nervous, but maybe it was the fact they'd been friends for years. Maybe it was that she knew him and trusted him. Maybe it was that she knew there was no way what they were about to do could let her down. What they were about to do would be nothing short of magical.

He eased into her slowly, a fierce look of concentration on his face. She pressed her hips up again, not wanting him to go slowly. She wanted all of him. Now.

"God," he breathed, then buried his head in her neck and held perfectly still.

She ran her hands over his back, just reveling in the feel of him inside her. She wanted to tell him how this felt. Wanted to let him know how perfect this was for her.

She couldn't find the words. With another moan, she began to circle her hips. It wasn't even a conscious decision to move. Her body needed it, demanded it.

"Christ, Cora," he swore but he pulled out of her before plunging back in, deep long strokes that drew her panting to a frenzy.

They didn't last long. Her orgasm was crashing over her, through her, in waves and he joined her, plunging deeper, harder.

They lay in a tangled heap, trying to catch their breath. She was doing more than that. She was trying to catch her breath, her heart, her everything.

When their breathing had returned to normal, Justin slid from the bed and went to the bathroom. She assumed he was taking care of the condom.

She closed her eyes, a smile still playing across her lips. She'd be smiling for a long time to come, she thought.

The mattress shifted and she opened her eyes to see Justin grinning at her. She liked seeing him smile so much. It was a good change.

He pulled open the bed stand drawer again and pulled out the small pad she'd used to write his bucket list.

Cora watched as he took a pen and wrote something then crossed it out.

He handed it to her.

He'd written, *make love to Cora* on the pad, then crossed it off.

CHAPTER TWENTY-SEVEN

CORA PULLED up to Ethan's house. It was hard not to think about the last time she'd come here, when it was Mr. Knight's house. Hard not to picture that moment when she'd found Mr. Knight on the floor.

She swallowed down the sadness and got out of the car. She would be meeting Justin for dinner in an hour but she wanted to see if Ethan was doing okay. She hadn't talked to him since the funeral.

Ethan's truck was out front. She hesitated when she saw another truck parked beside his. She could come back later, but she thought maybe it would be weird to pull in the driveway, then pull back out without at least saying hello.

She had made it to the front porch before she heard the yelling. Ethan and another man were fighting.

"I'm getting the hell out of here!" Ethan sounded mad, but there was a thread of fear under the anger. Cora didn't know which of those things scared her more. He didn't sound at all like the man she'd dated only weeks before.

Another man was saying something about having to

take care of it—whatever *it* was—but Cora didn't stick around to listen.

She didn't know what they were fighting about, but she knew it wasn't something she wanted to be involved with.

Cora turned and walked back down the steps quietly. Something told her to be as quiet as she could. That she didn't want to be caught here. Call it instinct, or maybe something as simple as gut self-preservation. She wanted out of there, now.

Ethan's panicked response followed her down the stairs. "We can't fix this. People are dead. *My dad* is dead, Derrick!"

She bolted for the car. She was halfway there she heard a shout. She didn't process much after that. There was the sound of the front door, boots on the steps, then a powerful arm around her waist.

It lifted her off the ground.

"No!" Cora cried out. A hand crushed her mouth. Something told her this wasn't Ethan. The feeling wasn't right. This person was bigger, stronger.

Meaner, a voice in her head offered.

She tried to lower her center of gravity, to spread her weight out and stabilize herself so she could fight back. She was slow. The things Justin had made her practice didn't come to her readily. Her brain and her body both seemed to be slogging through tar to make any movements.

She balled her hand into a fist and braced her thumb against her other fingers, making it as strong and rigid as she could. She plunged her fist, the nail of her thumb facing back, aiming for where her attacker's face should be.

A loud howl sounded and his grip slipped, but he didn't let go completely.

Then she heard Ethan yelling. There were muffled

movements. A loud crack. Something about the sound was sickening, and as the arms and weight of the person who'd grabbed her fell away from her, she realized what it must be. She realized Ethan had hit the other man.

Cora turned and saw Derrick Ayers lying on the ground at her feet. His head was bleeding and Ethan was holding a heavy shovel.

He came to her, hands on her arms. "Are you okay? Did he hurt you, Cora?"

Cora stammered, stunned at what had just happened. "N-no. I, I'm okay, I think."

Ethan looked back to Derrick's crumpled form, then to her. "We have to go."

He took her arm and led her to his truck. Cora stumbled, running to keep up with him. Yes, she thought. They needed to get to a safe spot where they could call for help.

He opened the truck and helped her in before running around to the driver's side.

Cora slumped in the seat next to him as he pulled down the long drive of his father's house. Her hands were shaking, but she was okay. They would get to safety and call for help.

CHAPTER TWENTY-EIGHT

ETHAN TURNED RIGHT, heading away from town. Cora turned in her seat to look back up the driveway. She saw no movement. No truck following them. She didn't think Derrick had tried to get up yet.

"He's not following us. We should be safe to call the police from here," she said.

Ethan shot her a look but didn't stop.

Cora waited a beat, turning again to look back at the house. Why was Ethan moving away from town? Shouldn't they be headed toward people, not away from them?

"Ethan, stop." Her voice still held the tone of someone who didn't understand what was going on. Someone who expected him to listen.

It was dawning on her, though, that he wasn't going to listen. He wasn't planning to call the police and explain what had happened. He wasn't planning to tell them that he'd had to hit Derrick because he was hurting Cora. It was the truth, but there was something else Ethan would have to admit to if he did. And he wasn't planning to tell anyone the truth.

Cora didn't want to know what it was. She just wanted to get out of the truck.

"Stop the truck, Ethan. Let me out."

His hands tightened on the wheel. "We just have to figure this out. We need to figure out some kind of story."

"There doesn't need to be a story," she said, in a measured calm tone. "You had to hit Derrick. He was hurting me. That's all we need to tell them. No one's going to blame you for that."

Ethan blew out a harsh breath and shoved a hand through his hair. His hand was shaking and he didn't look her way. His eyes stayed locked on the road ahead of them. It was an empty road now. Around his house, there might have been the chance of another person coming down the road, but now they'd gotten to the point where the cars would be few and far between.

"I just need to think, Cora. I'm going to figure this out."

Cora thought back to all she knew about being in a situation like this. It wasn't just what Justin had told her over the last few days. Her sister, Ashley, had been kidnapped once. That had been an eye-opening experience for all of them. Cora had read as much as she could after that about what to do if she was ever kidnapped.

She didn't consider this a kidnapping, really. Ethan likely hadn't stopped to think about what he was doing. What she needed to figure out, was how to get through to him. How to get him to realize what he was doing. If she could get him to stop and think, surely he wouldn't hurt her. He would let her go.

Should she yell at him and tell him to stop the car right now and let her out? He'd shown some protectiveness back there when he'd saved her from Derrick. But would that streak continue if he felt like she was turning on him?

Justin's voice came through to her. "Humanize yourself. Always make sure an abductor sees you as a person. If they do anything to make you think they're not seeing you that way anymore—if they stop feeding you, or cover your face up, or won't look at you—you fight like hell. Until then, stay calm and humanize yourself as much as possible until you see an opening to get help or get away."

Cora turned toward Ethan in the seat. "Thank you for stopping him. I was really scared when he grabbed me." No need to lie there. It was the truth and the shakiness in her voice as she relived that moment was genuine.

Her purse and her phone were in her car, but she had her keys in the pocket of her sweatshirt. Thanks to Justin, the keychain had a canister of pepper spray on it.

"We just need to figure this out," he said again. He seemed locked on that idea.

"Tell me what we need to figure out, Ethan."

"I didn't mean for any of this to happen. This was never supposed to be this way. I haven't gambled since I got out of this fucking town ten years ago. I did what I had to do to settle the debt before I left. It wasn't supposed to come back on us like this."

Cora froze, listening as Ethan talked.

He turned to her. "I just need to find a way to fix this."

"Fix what, Ethan?" She could spray him with the pepper spray but then he might crash the car. The stuff was strong and he was going fifty-five or sixty. An accident at this speed could kill them or at the very least, do a lot of damage.

He looked over at her again and then shook his head. "Derrick and I both owed people a lot of money. It wouldn't have worked if we didn't both plan it together. It only worked because I worked for the transport company and he worked for the company that was hired to dispose of the chemicals. With both of us on either end, we could change the paperwork to make sure the numbers matched up. I delivered some of the drums Caufield's sent and we buried the rest on my family's land. Derrick's sister worked in the billing department at the disposal company. She billed the amount Caufield's expected to pay, then only transmitted enough to cover what we said they sent. We kept the extra money."

Cora realized what he was saying. He and Derrick had buried those chemical drums the kids had discovered. They were the reason Mr. Knight and the kids had gotten sick.

She spoke quietly and calmly. "Derrick, just pull over and let me out. I'll walk back."

He didn't seem to hear. "Cora, you know me. You know I would never have done any of this on purpose. I never meant for any of this to happen."

Her other option was to jump from the car. But they were going too fast.

She could try to spray him with the pepper spray and grab the wheel, but she couldn't work the pedals. If she sprayed him, he could as easily hit the gas as he could the brake.

Maybe she could get him to pull over so they could talk.

"Ethan," she said, putting her hand on his arm very gently. Just the smallest touch to see if she could get through to him. "Pull the truck over so we can figure this out, Ethan. We need to stop and think before we go further. It's not a good idea to just run blindly."

He glanced her way, then nodded. He pulled the truck over to the side of the road and shifted into neutral.

Cora reached for the door. She was getting out of the truck before it started moving again.

She heard Ethan yell as she bolted.

"Cora, wait!"

Cora turned and faced Ethan. He stopped and stood in the headlights of the truck. It was getting dark out now.

Her hand was on the pepper spray as she talked to Ethan.

"I'm not getting back in the truck with you, Ethan. We can talk about this, but I'm not getting back in the truck." She still hoped she could talk him into calling the police and explaining things. She didn't want to mention the police yet. It was possible he would see that as a threat and things would escalate even more than they had. As far as she could tell, he still saw her as a potential ally.

He took a step closer, but she held out her hand and took a step back.

"Cora, I can't let anyone find out what we did. I need to get out of here. They'll figure it out and I can't be here when they do."

She gripped the canister of pepper spray and slid the safety lock to the side with her thumb so she was ready to use it if she had to. "I'm not going with you, Ethan. If you want to run, you're going to have to do it without me."

She didn't know how many miles they had travelled. Not many, she thought. Maybe five or so miles.

She nodded to the truck, hoping he would get in and go. If she stayed on the road, she could find her way to a house. They had passed a ranch house a mile or so back. It was dark, but she could stick to the road and find her way.

Ethan looked smaller somehow now, like he'd lost his way. "Just come with me. Please, Cora." He didn't seem to want her as a hostage. He almost seemed like he just didn't want to be alone in this.

He came toward her and reached for her, but she pulled

away. Anger crossed his features, made all the more vivid and frightening in the light of the headlights. "Cora, we have to go!"

She dodged his grip and brought the pepper spray up, aiming toward his face and pressing the trigger. She didn't know how accurately she hit him, but his scream told him she at least caused some amount of pain. He stopped and bent, hands to his face.

Cora didn't wait to see what would happen next. She ran to the truck and got in, shutting the doors and locking them.

Then she looked down and reality hit her. She didn't know how to drive a stick shift.

She looked up in time to see Ethan coming toward her. His eyes were nearly closed, blue ink streaked his face. A face now contorted with pain and rage. And she'd just trapped herself.

CHAPTER TWENTY-NINE

JUSTIN WAS LATER GETTING home than he'd planned. He had told Cora he wouldn't make it home in time for them to have dinner together, but he wanted to at least call her and maybe go over and spend some time with her if she was still awake.

He got out of the shower and tried her phone again. She hadn't answered his first call and she wasn't answering this one either. She'd said she was going to see Ethan. As much as Justin wanted to support her in that, he had to admit there was a small caveman part of him that wanted to grunt and groan about her going to see someone she'd just stopped dating.

He got dressed and tried to kill time, flipping through the channels looking for something to watch on TV. Cora was right. He needed a dog. His house was entirely too empty and quiet.

He picked up his phone and looked at it again to be sure he hadn't missed her call. Nothing.

It rang in his hand as he was setting it down, but when

he looked at it, he saw Ashley's name in the contact, not Cora's.

"Hey, Ashley, what's up?"

Ashley snorted. "Tell my sister she flaked on me."

"Sorry. She's not with me. Was she supposed to be with you?" Cora hadn't mentioned seeing Ashley, but it wasn't like he kept tabs on her every move.

"She's not with you?" Ashley didn't sound overly worried. More annoyed than anything.

"My car is in the shop and Garrett is on duty so she said she'd pick me up at the library. She didn't answer her phone so I figured she was with you."

"She went out to Ethan's to check on him, but," Justin checked the clock on the microwave, "that was three hours ago. What time did she say she'd pick you up?"

Ashley hesitated. "It was actually an hour ago. I just thought she would get to me eventually, so I've been catching up on work."

"I'll run out and check on her. Maybe Ethan's just really upset about his dad and she just hasn't felt right leaving him alone." Even as Justin said the words, he had a feeling she wouldn't have stayed with Ethan if it meant leaving Ashley stranded at the library. She would have at least called or texted Ashley to say she was running late or couldn't come. "Do you want me to swing by and get you?"

No," Ashley said. "I'll text Laura. I'd rather you head right out to check on her. Will you let me know when you track her down?"

"I will."

Justin grabbed his wallet and keys and headed for the door. Ethan's father's house was about twenty minutes away, but he could shave that to fifteen.

CHAPTER THIRTY

CORA SEARCHED the cab of the truck for a phone. Hers was in her car, but maybe Ethan had his in his truck.

Ethan pounded on the driver's side window. "Cora, open the door!"

Our heroine is not an idiot. God, she wished the narrator would shut up.

He stopped, coughing and spitting onto the pavement.

She opened the glove compartment. No phone. No weapon.

"Open this fucking door!" He kicked at the door. "Fuck!"

Cora took a slow, deep breath. At this point, would he let her go if she ran? She could get out of the passenger side door and run for the woods. She still had the pepper spray so she could hit him with that again, but she didn't know if that would do anything more at this point. She really had no idea.

Maybe now that he knew she was going to fight him, he'd rather get away in the truck than come after her. It was a gamble, but it was one she had to take. It was that or stay in the car and hope someone came along to help her. So far, there hadn't been anyone.

Ethan turned toward the woods on his side of the car and started looking for something. She could guess he was looking for something to help him break the window. That made the decision for her. Cora turned and released the locks while his back was to her. She bolted for the woods and ran.

CHAPTER THIRTY-ONE

JUSTIN FOUGHT BACK the sickening feeling as he tore through Ethan's house. There was blood on the flagstone walkway out front and it was obvious there had been a struggle. The house was empty and Cora didn't answer him as he called out to her again and again.

Her car was out front. Ethan drove a truck, but there was no truck in sight.

Justin went back out to the front of the house and dialed Garrett directly. He filled him in and hung up. It would take several minutes for Garrett or any of his officers to get there. Justin rounded the house and looked across the field at the back of it. No sign of anyone there.

He jogged back around to the front of the house and went into the living room. He'd seen a gun cabinet on his first run through the house. He lifted the fire poker from the fire place and crossed to the gun cabinet and broke through the glass. He lifted a rifle from the cabinet and headed out to his car. He would call Garrett and let him know he was heading out to look for her. Sitting and waiting for the police wasn't an option.

Justin thought as he pulled down the driveway. It was possible they'd headed toward town and he simply hadn't seen them on his way to the house. If something bad had happened and Cora was hurt, it either meant Ethan had been the one to hurt her or he was trying to help her. If he was trying to help her, he would have headed toward town with her. He'd get her to the hospital or the police station.

If that was the case, she'd be getting help already or would be getting it soon. If Ethan had been the one to hurt her, he would be heading away from the town center. He'd want to put distance between her and any help she could try to reach, wouldn't he?

Justin stopped for a second at the end of the driveway to text Garrett and let him know he was following the road away from town. If he didn't find anything, he could come back and join the search back here.

He put his phone on the dashboard and turned right. He had very little to go on, but it was better than sitting still and hoping Cora was all right.

He ignored the text from Garrett telling him to wait for the police to arrive. Justin wasn't an idiot. He knew what could happen to him. He'd been shot when he got between his sister-in-law and his brother's killer once. But he would gladly take another bullet if it meant keeping Cora safe.

He hoped like hell he was overreacting. Maybe there'd been an accident and someone was hurt. The blood might not even be Cora's. It could be Ethan and she'd driven him to the hospital.

Not likely, since she would have taken her own car if that was the case.

Still, maybe there was an accident and Ethan had taken Cora to the hospital and neither of them had been able to call and let anyone know.

Of course, the first thing Garrett would do was have one of his officers check with the hospital to see if anyone matching her description had been brought in. They would know in minutes if that was the case.

His car ate up the miles and there was no sign of Cora on the road.

Justin started to second guess himself. Maybe he should have gone on foot through the back field. Maybe Ethan was never home and that's why his truck wasn't there. It was possible someone else had been there and they'd hurt Cora. Could she have run out into the fields behind the house?

His mind made up all kinds of possibilities. But there were houses back behind Ethan's house. If she'd run that way, she would have been able to get to help, wouldn't she?

He lifted his foot from the gas, thinking he needed to turn around and head back.

He was seconds away from hitting the brake when he caught sight of something ahead. It was far out in the distance, but it was a truck. Justin couldn't remember what color Ethan's truck was, but this was the first sign of anyone out this way.

He hit the gas hard. If Cora was in trouble, he wouldn't waste any time getting to her.

CHAPTER THIRTY-TWO

CORA GULPED for breath as she ran. Running through the woods at night meant she couldn't move very quickly at all. But she had heard Ethan come after her as soon as he realized she'd taken off into the woods. She hoped he would give up when he realized they were getting further from the truck and his means of escape.

He'd alternated between cursing at her and attempting to cajole her into stopping so they could "just talk about it."

She pressed on, keeping one arm up over her face as she ducked tree limbs and tried to avoid being whipped in the face by saplings that were too thin to see easily in the dark.

She could hear Ethan coming closer and closer. She was running as hard as she dared through the trees, but he was closing the gap. She held the pepper spray as her mind scrambled through options. Could she find a large stick to defend herself with?

In all likelihood, anything she could swing wouldn't be large enough to hurt him, would it? Besides, stopping to look would probably give him too much time to get to her.

She chanced a look over her shoulder. He was close.

Too close. And if she kept running, she wouldn't have any energy left to fight him.

Cora turned and readied herself.

He was right there. He was on her.

She raised her hand and sprayed the pepper spray again, but he went for her arm this time. He slammed her arm into a tree, taking them both crashing down. She cried out in pain.

"Just listen to me, Cora!"

He had her pressed to the ground and he was still trying to reason with her. If she wasn't so terrified she would have laughed. Some part of her that felt like she was watching this from a distance almost did laugh.

She grabbed for anything around her. There were no rocks. Nothing large she could hit him with. His weight was so heavy.

She closed her fists around the leaves and dirt of the forest floor and raked her hands over his face with the mess. His eyes were sore and swollen already. When she pressed her hands into them and raked down, he howled in pain again and she bucked with her hips, trying to throw him off of her.

She put her hands together, making one large fist with them and struck at the side of his head, trying to throw him off balance. If she could just throw him off balance, maybe she could run again.

CHAPTER THIRTY-THREE

THE TRUCK WAS STOPPED on the side of the road, the passenger door open. Headlights on and the dome light in the cab glowing. It was empty.

Justin took only the time he needed to text Garrett and then he grabbed the rifle and a flashlight from his glove compartment and entered the woods on the passenger side of the truck.

"Cora!" He called out to her as he swept the light from left to right and back again in front of him. "Cora!"

Muffled shouts and the sounds of a fight met his ears. He broke into a run. She was there. She was fighting. He heard a shout of pain and it wasn't from Cora.

But Ethan was on top of her, pinning her down.

Justin saw red. He lifted the rifle and slammed the stock into the side of Ethan's head.

The man fell to the left and Justin put himself between Cora and her attacker.

"Are you okay, Cora?" he called.

"Yes." Her answer was shaky, quiet.

Justin turned to look at her. Ethan came up, flying at Justin.

Cora screamed.

Justin turned and blocked Ethan's swing, but the rifle went flying.

Ethan came at Justin again, a growl coming from him as he launched himself at Justin. Both men landed on the ground, Ethan on top.

Ethan threw punch after punch at Justin. They weren't landing hard, but they were landing. Justin leaned up, grabbing Ethan around the waist and pulling him down to him, gripping him tight so they were close together. It gave Ethan very little chance to throw any more punches and took him off balance.

Justin trapped Ethan's leg with his own, crossed over his shoulder and flipped Ethan to his back. An elbow and a punch to the face finished the job.

Ethan was out.

Justin stood and lifted the rifle in one hand as he pulled Cora to him with his other arm. They heard sirens approaching on the road.

"Are you okay?" He asked the question again, even though she'd already said she was.

Justin couldn't see her well enough to check her for wounds, but he ran his hands over her.

"I'm okay," she said, as she burrowed closer, wrapping her arms around him. Nothing had ever felt better to him.

Justin realized his heart was hammering in his chest. Hell, he didn't know what he would have done if he'd gotten here any later. He had no idea what the hell had happened. No clue why Ethan had gone after her, but he thanked God Ashley had called him and given him a reason to come out here and check on her.

"You fought," he said, pulling back and looking at her. "You ran and you fought and you hung on."

"I had it under control," she said, talking into his chest, her face buried against him.

Justin swore, then laughed, because there wasn't anything else he could do in that moment. He laughed and he kissed her and he held her to him as the police moved in to secure the scene.

CHAPTER THIRTY-FOUR

TWO HOURS LATER, they had the story. Ethan was in custody and Derrick Ayers had been caught when he'd walked into a clinic with a gash in his head. He didn't put up much of a fight when the police caught up with him there.

Ethan had come home to help his father, knowing he was likely responsible for the water poisoning that was causing his illness. When the chemical drums had been dug up and Caufield Furniture named the transport company responsible for shipping the drums to the disposal site, his father had put two and two together. He'd known Ethan and Derrick had worked for the two companies. The fact the drums were found on land that used to belong to the Knights was too much of a coincidence.

Ethan and his dad had fought. Ethan said he didn't push his dad down the stairs. In the heat of the argument, his father lost his balance and Ethan couldn't get to him in time to stop it.

He swore his dad was already dead when he left the house. He had planned to say he found him lying there when he got home, but forgot Cora came out most Sundays to see his father. Cora didn't know what to believe but that would be for a judge or a jury to figure out.

For now, she wanted to go home.

No, that wasn't true. She wanted to go wherever Justin would be.

Her family had other ideas. They were currently all packed into the Evers Police Department lobby.

"Really, mom, I'm okay."

Justin stood behind her, his hands on her shoulders, the firm pressure calming her. "I'll get her home, Mrs. Walker."

"She should have someone stay with her tonight," Cora's mom said. "She shouldn't sleep alone."

"I think he's got that covered, too, mom," Ashley said.

Cora flushed but Justin squeezed her shoulders again and she had a feeling he was trying not to laugh.

In the end, she went home with Justin to his house, preferring his larger bed. They stopped at her house for her to grab her toothbrush and a change of clothes.

He flipped the lights on in his bedroom when they finally made it to his place. "Do you want me to make you some tea? Or hot chocolate?"

"No. I want you next to me."

He nodded and slipped into the bed next to her, pulling her against him.

She snuggled in, needing the warmth and strength of his arms around her. "I heard your voice in my head when I was in the truck with him. I heard you coaching me on what to do and how to get away."

He kissed the top of her head, his arms wrapped around her. "I'm so damned glad you fought back. God, I don't know what I would have done if..."

He didn't finish the sentence. She shivered in his arms

at the thought of what might have happened if he didn't get there when he had. She had been running out of energy to fight and Ethan had been so much stronger than she was.

Justin held her through the night. She wasn't sure if he slept at all. She drifted in and out of sleep, often not sleeping for more than a few minutes, it seemed. She would jerk awake and Justin would be there to soothe her.

At some point, when the sky started to lighten in the morning, they both fell asleep for a little while. Cora woke more slowly that time. Maybe because it was daylight then.

She watched Justin sleep and felt herself relax. She felt the tension that had been with her, even in sleep, drain.

He opened his eyes. "Hey."

"Hey, yourself."

He made a show of looking around. "I thought for sure your father or brothers would show up to check on you in the middle of the night."

She laughed. "Nah, if anyone was that crazy, it would be my mom. Ashley probably had to hold her down."

"I know how they feel." He ran a large hand over her arm and up to her shoulder. "We'll let them get eyes on you again today, so they don't start to worry."

"Not yet," she said and wrapped her arms around his neck.

When they kissed, it was slow and deep, long. They were soothing kisses. The kind she needed right now. Justin spoke to her, as he ran his hands over her body.

There were promises in his words. Promises to keep her safe, to cherish her. Promises that he would come for her, always. That no matter what happened, he'd always protect her.

Cora couldn't touch him enough. She ran her hands

over his skin, through his hair, over his mouth. She wanted to feel all of him, to know she was there, alive and safe.

He made love to her slowly and gently.

When he was deep inside her, her arms and legs wrapped around him, he spoke. "You're everything to me, Cora."

She held his gaze. "I love you, Justin."

Truth burned in his eyes when he spoke. "I love you, Cora Walker." He began to move slowly with her again. "I love you with everything I am."

EPILOGUE

OUR HEROINE IS VERY, *very happy.*

This narrator wasn't getting any better with time, but he was accurate. Cora was very, very happy.

She watched as Ashley opened her baby shower gifts. It was a co-ed shower so Justin stood behind her, his arm wrapped around her holding her to him. They stood to one side, joining the crowd in the oooing and aaahing that was happening with each gift.

Cora turned and grinned up at Justin. He smiled back and dropped a kiss to the top of her head.

She loved that he looked so much more relaxed than he used to. She still had that *pinch me, this can't be real* thing going on whenever she thought about the fact she and Justin were together. But, more than that, she was glad to see how much he'd changed in the last six months.

He still worked a lot. He was passionate about his work so it made sense that he'd want to devote time to that. Now, though, he took weekends and evenings off because they wanted to spend time together. He'd hired a deputy director at Raise the Veil and turned over a lot of his workload.

He had also gone back to taking martial arts and was teaching a self-defense class in town with Garrett every other month. They offered it free to anyone who wanted to attend.

"She looks beautiful, doesn't she?" Cora whispered to him. She thought Ashley really had that glow people talk about during pregnancy, even if her ankles were clearly swollen.

Justin leaned in and whispered in her ear. "She's as big as a house."

Cora elbowed him, drawing a laugh and an amended response.

"A beautiful house. She's an absolutely gorgeous pregnant house."

"Damned right." Cora turned back to watch Ashley open another of Cora's gifts. She might have gone a bit overboard.

Between her and the rest of the Walker siblings, Ashley wouldn't need to shop for this child.

Ashley opened the box and laughed, holding up a onesie that said "feed, burp, wipe, repeat."

Haddie sat on one side of Ashley in a T-shirt that read, *I might look young, but I'm the honorary grandmother*.

Laura was sitting on the other side of Ashley, with Cade behind her on the couch. She pointed at the onesie. "I want that one when you're done with it."

She'd said that for nearly every cute onesie Ashley had gotten. Laura and Cade were expecting another baby four months after Ashley's due date. Cora suspected Katelyn was pregnant, too, but since she and John hadn't said anything yet, no one was talking about it.

Babies were in the air in Evers. Cora looked around the room. Carter and Lilly sat on one side of the room.

They were married now and she wondered if they might be next.

Phoebe and Shane were there, as were Gina and the General. General Brophy had retired. He had moved to town and he and Gina were officially an item, which was beyond adorable, Cora thought.

Presley and James had made an appearance for the baby shower. Even though he stayed close to the door most of the time, his back to the wall, he was talking and laughing with the other guests.

Cora looked around. The room was filled with all the people she loved. Her parents and sisters and brothers. Her friends. They were people she cherished in her life, and she knew she didn't need to worry that they would leave her.

Yes, some might move away. Others were growing older and wouldn't be with them all forever. At times, things would change, but that was part of life. She was okay with that, now. She would live for the moment and focus on what made her so blessed in life, not what might happen someday.

The somedays could swallow you up if you let them.

———

JUSTIN PULLED Cora into his arms in his living room and kissed her, forcing himself to keep the kiss soft. He'd been dying to get her out of the baby shower but she'd been so happy, he hadn't suggested they leave until most of the guests had gone home.

Still, it was hard not to let himself do all he wanted to do to her right now. He had other plans for the evening, though. "Wait here for a minute?" He asked, leading her to the couch.

She gave him a questioning look, but nodded and sat. "Be right back."

He went down the hall to his bedroom and got the room ready. He'd had everything tucked away in one of the dresser drawers for a week now and he couldn't wait any longer.

He went back down the hall to find her craning her neck as though she might be able to see what he was doing.

She shot him a cheeky grin when she was caught.

It was crazy how nervous he was about this. It wasn't like he thought she'd say no, but still, he wanted everything to be perfect for her.

When she gasped as she entered the room, he knew he'd gotten it right. Small candles lit the room and dried jasmine buds Presley had gotten for him covered the duvet on the bed. The scent filled the room. In the center lay the notebook she'd written his bucket list in. He'd added *Marry Cora* and *Make Cora Happy for the Rest of Our Lives* to the list.

She covered her mouth with her hands, tears making her brown eyes glisten in the candle light.

Justin dropped to one knee and pulled the ring box from his pocket. "Cora, I don't even have words to tell you what you've done for me, what loving you means to me. There's no way for me to tell you what you've given me. So much was missing from my life, but it's all there now. Love, happiness, family. All of it. You're already everything to me. Will you be my wife?"

She didn't say anything. She dropped to her knees and kissed him. She was crying and not talking, but he got the sense they were good tears and this was the *yes* kind of kneeling and kissing going on.

He kissed her back, pulling her into his arms and cherishing her. He'd meant what he said. There was no way to explain what she meant to him, but he might be able to make her feel it in his kiss. If not, he'd spend the rest of his life trying to show her.

And then she was saying *yes* over and over against his mouth as they kissed and he knew the only thing that might ever top this day would be their wedding. Or maybe the birth of their first child. Or maybe all of the other things he wanted to share with her.

———

THANK you so much for reading my Heroes of Evers, TX series! Someday, I might come back to this world and write in it again. For now, that's the end. But if you love my books and want to read more, I recommend checking out The Billionaire Deal, book one in my Sutton Billionaires Series. It's contemporary romance with a suspense twist. Grab it here: loriryanromance.com/book/the-billionaire-deal

Read on for chapter one of The Billionaire Deal:

———

CHAPTER ONE

W*HISH, swoosh, whish, swoosh, whish, swoosh.*

Jack Sutton lost himself in the rhythmic sound of the churning wheels of his bike as he rounded the final bend of an eight-mile morning ride.

He was flanked by his cousin, Chad, who was more like a brother to him than a cousin, and their best friend, Andrew. The three met once or twice a month to ride next to the Long Island Sound where Jack's home was located.

Jack saw Chad soar past him out of the corner of his eye

as he raced the last few yards ahead of him and Andrew, cutting into Jack's driveway to easily take the lead. It never ceased to amaze Jack.

Chad had a good three inches over Jack's tall frame, and he was built like a military tank. The man shouldn't be able to move the way he did, but he was still somehow faster and more agile than both Andrew and Jack.

Jack and Andrew exchanged a look, grinning at Chad's need to beat them every time they rode. Most days, Andrew and Jack would at least give Chad a fight over the winning slot, but beating Chad wasn't on Jack's mind today, and he had a feeling it wasn't on Andrew's either.

The showdown he would have with Chad's mother— Jack's Aunt Mabry—later today was what had him tense and uneasy. He had hoped the morning ride would take the edge off, but it hadn't helped.

He shoved aside his mood long enough to put on a show for Chad while the three men rode slow laps through the circular drive to cool down, each one sipping water and talking trash as they rode. He'd be damned if he'd let Chad see anything was wrong. He wouldn't make his cousin choose a side no matter what Mabry threw at him.

It wasn't until after Chad loaded up his bike and pulled out of the driveway that Jack raised the subject they'd been avoiding for the last couple of hours.

"Spill it," Jack said. Andrew had been grinding his jaw the whole ride, so he knew whatever he'd been avoiding saying in front of Chad wasn't good.

Andrew was one of a handful of people who knew Chad's mother was finally making good on her threat to try to take over the company Jack's father had built. The terms of Jack's mother's will were going to let her take control of a large portion of the shares of Sutton Capital, and vote Jack out of his position as Chief Executive Officer.

She wanted Chad to take Jack's place at the head of the board table and she was willing to do whatever it took to see that happen.

Jack and Andrew had been quietly approaching the shareholders in the privately-owned company to be sure Jack had their support if Mabry got her hands on the stock his mother had once controlled.

Andrew didn't blink when he looked at Jack and broke the news. "John Barton died of a heart attack last night."

Jack swallowed a curse and swiped his face with his hand. "He wasn't very old at all. When did it happen?" he asked, shock hitting him like a sledge hammer.

"Sixty-seven and supposed to be retired, but he didn't know the definition of the word. I don't think the man has taken a vacation in twenty years, but Anne finally talked him into going to Italy. They were supposed to leave in three days for a two-week vacation and then this happens."

The two men were silent for a few minutes before Jack realized what this meant for his battle with Mabry.

Oh hell. He scrubbed a hand down his face. This could not be happening. "I know this isn't a great time to bring this up, but— " Jack began before Andrew cut in.

"But nothing. You have to think about the rest of the shareholders, the company, its employees—there's a lot at stake for a lot of people here, Jack. We need to figure out who will have control of Barton's shares, and find out what that does to our chances against your Aunt Mabry."

This time Jack didn't bother to swallow his curse. He let fly with a few words his mother would have been pissed to hear coming from his mouth.

"Grab a shower and meet me at the office," he said.

"We'll deal with this there." He didn't wait for an answer. He turned and took the front steps two at a time, hustling to get showered and dressed to deal with the latest catastrophe in his ongoing battle with his aunt.

GET THE BILLIONAIRE DEAL NOW! loriryanromance. com/book/the-billionaire-deal

If you want more of a police procedural feel, grab my Dark Falls or Pure Vengeance at loriryanromance.com.

ABOUT THE AUTHOR

Lori Ryan is a NY Times and USA Today bestselling author who writes romantic suspense, contemporary romance, and sports romance. She lives with an extremely understanding husband, three wonderful children, and two mostly-behaved dogs in Austin, Texas. It's a bit of a zoo, but she wouldn't change a thing.

Lori published her first novel in April of 2013 and hasn't looked back since then. She loves to connect with her readers.

For new release info and bonus content, join her newsletter here: loriryanromance.com/lets-keep-touch.

Follow her online:

facebook.com/loriryanromance

twitter.com/Loriryanauthor

instagram.com/loriryanauthor

Manufactured by Amazon.ca
Bolton, ON